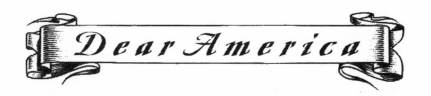

I Thought My Soul Would Rise and Fly

The Diary of Patsy, a Freed Girl

BY JOYCE HANSEN

Scholastic Inc. New York

Mars Bluff, South Carolina
1865

Friday, April 21, 1865

I am so frightened my heart is dancing a reel in my chest. I've never written in a book before. If Mistress Davis catch me she'll whip me and take you away, little book. She'll also take the pen and ink and say that I stole them. But I have not. Her own niece, Annie, gave you to me this morning as a joke. Annie and her brother Charles enjoy making fun of me. And it was Annie who taught me how to read as a joke as well, until Mistress made her stop.

"We are only playing school, Aunt," Annie would say. "Patsy isn't learning anything. She is the dunce, Charles is the smart pupil, and I am the teacher."

"That's not a proper game. Suppose one of our visitors sees you and misunderstands. It's illegal to teach slaves how to read and write. It spoils them."

But it was too late, for I had already learned how. Whenever newspapers was thrown away for burning I would take a page and hide it under my pallet, so that when I was alone, I could practice reading words. And whenever I was by the creek or in the kitchen garden, I would get a small stick that I used as a pen and practice writing letters in the dirt. I never let anyone know. Annie was a willful child, so we never stopped playing the game. And the more I played the dunce, the more I learned.

I've been tending to Annie and Charles from the time their father, Master's brother, brought them to Davis Hall to live after their mother died. They were babies and I was but a little tot myself, maybe about three or four years old. I had to help one of the women, who was too old to work in the fields, take care of them. Serving Annie and Charles has been my task ever since.

This morning when Annie gave you to me, little book, she said, "Now that the War has ended, we are leaving South Carolina, Patsy. Charles and I can't carry all of our belongings so we are giving you this diary, ink, and a pen. You must write all of your beautiful thoughts in this book while we are gone." Annie and Charles laughed until tears ran down their cheeks. "Imagine a dunce having beautiful thoughts," Charles said.

I know what a dunce is, but I stared at them as if I didn't understand what they were saying. Then Charles stuck his book in my face. "Patsy," he said, "don't forget to put a date first each time you write your beautiful thoughts. Today is Friday, April 21, 1865. You must tell what happens in your life."

These are my thoughts. I don't suppose they are beautiful, but the joke is on Annie and Charles. They thought they were giving me something I couldn't use. Now I can write as Mistress Davis does in her book. I will keep track of all of my days.

Mostly, my thoughts are about where I've always lived here on the Davis Hall Plantation and how everything is changing and remaining the same all at once.

The grown-ups hold secrets, and whispers hang in the air like the strands of moss that dangle from some of the oak trees. All of Master's hounds was poisoned and the plantation jail and the whipping post was burned down. No one knows who did it. The grown-ups talk about the people who left Davis Hall last week — the carpenter, the cobbler, and the blacksmith.

Cook says that the Yankees won the War and that we are free. But Master and Mistress have not said a word about us being free. Cook is still cooking and complaining. She is so mean, one of these days she's going to cuss up her ownself. James is still taking care of Master. Does everything for him. When Master catch a cold, James be the one who sneeze. Nancy is still taking care of Mistress and following behind her like a noonday shadow. Ruth is still cleaning and making sure everything in the house is the way Mistress wants it. Miriam is still washing and ironing and gossiping with Cook. The field hands are still plowing and planting. I am still emptying chamber pots.

Little book, I hope you like your new home in my chamber, but it is merely a storeroom inside the kitchen shed. I moved myself in here last March. I used to sleep in one of the cottages that line the walkway leading to The House. The house slaves, carpenter, cobbler, blacksmith, and their families lived there, too, before we was freed. The field hands still live in cabins on the other side of the plantation, near the cotton fields.

I stayed in the same cottage with Cook, Ruth, her son Luke, and Miriam. Since there was only one room, I was rarely alone to practice my reading, and I was always afraid that Luke would discover the papers I'd hidden in the wheat straw under my pallet. He's only a little boy, about seven, and might tell my secret. If Master and Mistress find out that I can read, I might be whipped for sure.

The storeroom next to the kitchen shed has only a tin tub, some candle forms, a flax wheel, a rickety milking stool, and a box of scraps of cloth that we use for dust rags and patchwork quilts.

When I moved my pallet here, Cook said it was a good idea because I won't be late getting the fire started in the morning. There is a hook where I hang my one other homespun dress and my apron. And I can put my candle on the milking stool. So, my Friend, this is our chamber that we have all to ourselves. I hope no one finds you and takes you away from me.

I must go now. Cook is calling my name all over the yard.

Saturday, April 22, 1865
Sunrise

I want to tell you more about my life, but I must write quickly before Cook comes to the kitchen. I started the fire even before the cock crowed, so I wouldn't have to listen to Cook's mouth.

Writing to you is like speaking to a friend, so I shall call you Dear Friend, since I don't have any real friends, except Luke. But I can't speak to him the way I would talk with a girl my own age. He is a nice boy, though, and treats me as if there's nothing wrong with me.

Nancy and I are about the same age, but I don't like her. She try to play the mistress with me. Miriam, James, and Cook hardly know I am around, except to tell me when I've made a mistake or to shush me when I try to speak. Master and Mistress only speak to me to give me an order.

Ruth, Luke's mother, is almost like a friend. She has always been kind to me. She never yells or tells me to hush up or talks for me.

You see, Friend, I have a problem. When I write to you the words come out easily, not the way I stammer and sputter when I speak, which is why I am so silent most of the time and people think I am dim-witted.

Yesterday Mistress told me that since Annie and Charles are gone I have to help Cook all day. In the past, I was only with Cook in the mornings and evenings. I would light the coals, fetch water for cooking, and sometimes knead dough for biscuits, or make coffee out of sweet potatoes. There has been no real coffee to buy because of the War.

This is how I turn sweet potatoes into coffee: First I cut the potatoes into small chips, then dry them in the sun, and next I parch them on the hot coals and grind them so that they are just like coffee grains. Cook taught me how to do this. Master hates it and cusses up Yankees every time he drinks it.

In the mornings, when the last patches of dark disappear, James, Ruth, Miriam, Cook, and I sit on the benches in front of the large pine table in the kitchen shed and eat cornbread or biscuits, sometimes grits, and at special times eggs. We wash our food down with a cool glass of milk. Nancy eats later, by herself at the table, because she has to comb Mistress's hair and help her dress. Nancy sleeps in The House at the foot of Mistress's bed. James sleeps in The House, too. Only he has his own servant's room. So James must be higher up than Nancy is. He sleeps in a four-poster bed; Nancy sleeps on a pallet. Are you laughing, Friend? I am.

When we finish breakfast, it's time for all of us to do our tasks. I help Ruth serve Master and Mistress their breakfast, and also help her clean a little.

That is how we lived before freedom. We're still living almost the same way except, Annie and Charles are gone.

I must go now. If there is time, I will talk with you later.

Evening

I found a piece of candle, so I can write to you once again, Friend. Cook is the evilest woman in the world sometimes. Nothing pleases her. This afternoon she said the gingerbread dough I kneaded was too lumpy, and the oak chips and bark I collected for her cooking fire were not dry enough. Maybe she is disturbed over the news that James told her this morning. The Yankee President Lincoln was killed a week ago. James and Cook both seem worried. Cook said, "Maybe we not free then, since the man who free us is dead."

When I helped Ruth serve Master and Mistress their breakfast this morning, Master called the dead President a black Republican and said that he was vulgar and uncouth like all Yankees. What is vulgar and uncouth? I wonder. It don't sound so nice. I've never seen a Yankee; none ever came here during the War. Though I heard James and Cook say once that sometimes Yankee soldiers tore up homes and plantations. Maybe that be uncouth.

Charles and Annie said that Yankees have horns and tails, but I don't believe that. I think they are human people. Charles and Annie always try to make me believe any fool thing they say.

I've been thinking, if I am free what will my life

be like? I wonder. Can I have real school lessons like Annie and Charles?

Dear Friend,

I wish Annie and Charles had not left because now there are no more lessons. You see, I'd be helping Ruth, and I'd make sure I was dusting in Master's library where Annie and Charles were with their teacher. I'd dust very slowly, so I could hear how they learned to read and write. One of my legs is shorter than the other, so I don't move as fast as most people, but I dragged my bad leg slow as a turtle crossing a road so I could listen to those lessons.

Then I'd make believe I was too fool to leave the room when I finished dusting and sit on the rug near the door and stare blankly as if I didn't know my own name. When the teacher wrote letters on the slate that hung over the desk, I'd form letters in the dust on the floor and wipe it off before anyone saw me. Most of all I liked to hear the story about Marygold in *A Wonder Book for Girls and Boys*, but my favorite is *The History of Little Goody Two-Shoes* because the girl in the story is like me and has no mother and no father, and taught herself how to read and write. I have shoes though. The cobbler made slippers for all of us who work in The House.

I don't know who my mother or father is. No one has ever told me my history. I wonder if either one had a bad leg like me, or if people called them slow. I wonder sometimes if I ever had a mother or father — maybe God spit me out and I got this bad leg when I fell to the ground. Are you laughing, Friend? I am. I don't know how old I am, but I think I'm twelve or thirteen, since Annie is ten and Charles is nine.

I must leave now, Friend. I have to put on my other homespun dress that I wear on Sundays. Nancy, me, James, and Miriam always go to church with Master and Mistress. I wish I could take you with me. Father Holmes will surely put me to sleep.

Everyone else goes to the bush arbor near the cabins where the field hands have their own church services outside under the arbor. I have never gone to church down there because Master and Mistress insist I go with them. But I like to hear the singing that comes from the arbor on Sundays. Some Sundays Master and Mistress do not attend church, so Nancy and I don't go either, and if I listen hard, I can faintly hear the field hands singing.

Monday, April 24, 1865

Dear Friend,

I saw Yankees for the first time today when I was carrying milk from the dairy house. I tried to see why Master calls them vulgar and uncouth, but I still don't understand. They look no different from the white men I have always seen. They didn't have no horns either. Friend, I can't say whether or not they had tails. I thought it would be rude to ask.

Early this morning three of them rode up the drive leading to The House. When the soldiers reached the cottages, they stopped their horses. Master and Mistress seemed small and old, but they held their heads as high as the pine trees surrounding The House. They talked to the soldiers at length, but I do not know what was said.

While I was sweeping the passageway that separates the kitchen from The House, Master called everyone, including the field hands, to the yard. He stood between the gleaming white columns of The House as he talked to us. "The government says I have to pay you wages now. If you remain, your pay will be one tenth of the cotton crop you bring in, and you can live in your same cabins."

Then he looked at James, Cook, and Ruth and said, "I will pay you ten dollars a month and provide food as in the past." He didn't say anything to Nancy or Miriam — much less me. Maybe because we are the youngest of the house slaves.

One of the Yankee soldiers spoke next. I had to listen closely to understand his words for his speech sounded so different from ours, as if he was talking through his nose.

He explained that he is from some place called the Freedmen's Bureau and that the Bureau is helping former slaves adjust to being free. "You must behave yourselves and work as you are accustomed. All field hands must sign a yearly work contract. Anyone found roaming about the countryside without a job or a place to live will be arrested for vagrancy."

Everyone was silent. I counted eighty field hands, men and women, and not a one was smiling. Even the birds stopped singing. Then one of the hands named Douglass spoke. Douglass used to always do chores for Mistress at special times, like take down the drapes when it was time for cleaning The House for Christmas. He was a boy then, but now he is a thin, handsome young man and works in the fields with his mother and sister. "Sir," Douglass said. "Tell me one thing. Is we free?"

Then other people started calling out, too. The Yankee shushed them. He told us that we are free, but whoever doesn't work and follow the rules will be jailed. He says we are not free to roam about and cause trouble.

Then the man everyone calls Brother Solomon, because he does the preaching in the arbor on Sundays, spoke to the soldier. "Sir, we will not stay here 'less we get a school for our young ones and land for us to farm for our own selves."

Master turned a slow red and Mistress stared at Brother Solomon with angry gray eyes. I was surprised to see her look at him that way. She and Master always said he was the best hand they had. Brother Solomon is headman over the field hands and helps the overseer. He also makes sure the gardens and the orchards are taken care of.

Master said to Brother Solomon that if they stay, he will give each family five acres of land and a plantation school. The hands smiled and so did I. Imagine a school on Davis Hall Plantation.

But one of the elderly women, her hands shaking as she held on to her walking stick, asked what would happen to the old people who can't bring in a crop anymore. She began to cry and she made me almost cry as well.

One of the soldiers spoke before Master answered and told her that elderly people cannot be thrown off farms and plantations. Master has a responsibility to care for them.

Then Brother Solomon spoke to the woman. "Mother Naomi, we all in this cauldron together. We take care of you."

Friend, if I was a brave girl, I'd have asked that Yankee whether I would be punished if I limped on upstairs to Master's library and started reading and writing. Master never did say we was free, but I guess we are. I can't wait until we get a school. I'll be the first pupil there.

Tuesday, April 25, 1865

Dear Friend,

I woke up this morning thinking about school. Will Mistress let me go? I wonder.

When we were eating breakfast, James began to talk about names. He said now that we was free we had to have last names. Cook said she would take her father's name, George, for her last name. Ruth took Luke's father's name. His name is John, and

Luke is John's son, so they will have the last name of Johnson.

Miriam said that she would not choose a last name until she saw her mother again. Her mother lives on Master's other plantation on Edisto Island.

Ruth asked me what name I would take. I shrugged my shoulders. I started to answer, but Cook spoke for me, like always, instead of letting me finish.

"She'll be Davis. Most of these people will take the name Davis, especially them ones who always been here."

Now I have something else to think about along with school. I will not take the name Davis. That's Master and Mistress's name. I will take my time and pick a beautiful name for myself. A name of my own.

Wednesday, April 26, 1865

Dear Friend,

Instead of helping Cook, Mistress told me to help Ruth clean inside the house. I was glad, for Ruth is not as miserable as Cook is. It is Ruth and James who make sure that everything in The House is in order.

As I swept out Annie's chamber, I heard Ruth humming while she worked in the dining room. I guessed that she was in a happy mood so I found the courage to ask her whether I could dust in the library when I finished in the chamber.

I went first to the partner's desk where Annie and Charles used to sit, facing each other, and reading together. I didn't see any of their books. My heart sank. They must have taken them all. I had to content myself with dusting Master's and Mistress's books on the shelves and reading the titles. I hoped maybe I would find a name for myself on one of the books.

They did leave their magazine, *The Youth's Companion*, on the desk, and when I picked it up, I found my favorite book, *Little Goody Two-Shoes*, under it.

I dusted part of the desk with one hand and turned the pages of the book with the other. If anyone came in, I was going to pretend to be dusting. Time flew. I was startled when I heard Ruth say, "You not finished yet?" She wiped her hands across the dust on top of the piano.

"You so slow, gal, and what you doing with that book? You can't read it. I'm getting Nancy to come in here and finish."

Well, my Friend, you know how I talk. "I-I-I'm

s-s-sorry," I sputtered and got to moving faster than I thought I could. Then I told her that Nancy was busy fixing Mistress's hair. She let me stay and I contented myself with reading titles again while I dusted. I've often noticed *A Christmas Carol* by Charles Dickens and wonder what it is about. But I didn't dare take it off the shelf.

It's lucky that Mistress didn't catch me reading. But if I am free, then must I hide my reading and writing? Somehow I don't think I am free or anybody else is. All of us in The House and in the fields are doing our same tasks. Who did the Yankees free? I wonder.

Thursday, April 27, 1865

Dear Friend,

There are about eighty hands to work hundreds of acres of land. Will they get through it all? I wonder. I heard Cook say that many people are starving now because the farms were ruined during the War. People have to live off food the Yankee soldiers give out. But the land on Davis Hall is plowed and the seeds are planted — cotton, corn, and potatoes are the main crops. There's a kitchen garden that Cook mostly looks after once Brother

Solomon has planted okra, peas, and greens. I don't think we will be starving.

Mistress is everywhere, looking, peeking, watching every move we make. Nancy always crows that she's Mistress's personal ladies' maid and flounces behind her as if she's a mistress, too. I haven't seen Master since the Yankees told us that we were some kind of free. But I know he is here because James shaved him this morning and made sure that Miriam ironed his shirts correctly.

I had a good laugh today. Mistress was in and out of the kitchen all morning with her pet Nancy, worrying Cook about fixing tasty treats. But Cook sassed her. "If you can tell me how to make a pecan pie out of hominy grits, then I'll make a pecan pie." I thought Mistress would slap her, but she turned as red as a beet and stomped away with Nancy flouncing behind her.

Cook sucked her teeth so loud, I thought that they'd pop out of her mouth. Maybe now Cook is free to sass Mistress to her face instead of complaining behind her back. Cook sent me to the icehouse to make sure there were no pecans left over from last year's supply. I hoped they weren't all gone. Cook makes the best pecan pie and always bakes one for us whenever she bakes one for the family.

I limped as fast as I could (which wasn't very fast) toward the peach and cherry orchards. They are full of weeds and only a few blossoms peek from among the leaves. Brother Solomon doesn't have anyone to help him tend the orchards as he used to. Many of the younger hands was forced to go with the Confederate soldiers to build forts and roads and work in their camps, and those who are left have to work the fields.

I remember the day the Confederates came and marched right down to the slave quarters to get the men they needed. That was three years ago. Master was upset because he had to give up his strongest slaves. I felt sorry for the women and children who cried so bitterly. That was when I first noticed Douglass because his mother held on to him so tight. But the soldiers didn't take him. He was only a skinny boy then, not as tall and handsome as he is now. Why am I thinking these thoughts?

The Confederate Army also got a share of the potatoes, corn, peas, and okra. Master had to give up some of his cattle, horses, and a mule. None of the men returned. Cook said they may have been killed in the War. I hope not.

The icehouse is just beyond the pond, near the dairy and smokehouse. When the pond freezes in the winter, the ice is collected and put into the deep hole inside the icehouse. I entered the house and lifted the cover over the hole. A ladder goes all the way to the bottom. All I saw was ice and several barrels of brandy, cider, pickles, and preserves. No pecans.

When I told Cook, she said, "Start kneading the gingerbread dough. You remember how I showed you?" I nodded, but imagined wrapping my lips around a sweet piece of pecan pie.

I found out why Mistress worried Cook about the food. Her cousin Sarah from Columbia is coming to stay for a spell. She and her husband lost their possessions in the fire that burned down the city two months ago.

Master say the Yankee devils did it. James say the Confederate soldiers burned it down when they realized that the Yankee General Sherman would capture the city. Why do people do such terrible things? I wonder. I hope that Miss Sarah has children old enough for school lessons.

I am still looking for a name.

Friday, April 28, 1865

Dear Friend,

There was such excitement and confusion today. As I was carrying the chamber pots I'd emptied back to The House, I saw Master charging along the passageway and into the kitchen shed. His britches were practically falling down, and his thick gray hair looked like a pile of hay. He shouted for James.

Cook walked slowly out of the kitchen. "Ain't seen him, Sir," she said. It was strange for James not to be there. Every morning God has sent, James has been here to dress Master, shave him, cut his hair, and make sure that everything runs smoothly in The House. James walks tall and straight as Master, as if he also owned Davis Hall Plantation. It felt as though everything was backwards without James to tell us how to do things right.

In the middle of all of the James confusion, Mistress's cousin Sarah and her two little children arrive. The children are only babies, so there will be no lessons.

When Ruth and I served the family at dinnertime, Master was not there. I guess he couldn't bear to eat at the table without James waiting on him. The children were in the drawing room with Nancy. Miss Sarah could hardly eat for talking. She rattled on how she and her husband lost all of their home in Columbia and their plantation on Edisto Island. "Imagine, Cousin," she said to Mistress. "This horrible Yankee military government we live under gave my land to my slaves." She began to cry and Mistress tried to comfort her.

When I carried their plates back to the kitchen shed, I was surprised to see Master eating there at the big, rough pine table where we eat. The only other time he ate in the kitchen shed was when he and Mistress had a fight. His plate was piled up with okra and rice. Maybe he thinks Cook knows where James is. She probably does, but she'd never tell.

Saturday, April 29, 1865

Dear Friend,

James is really gone, but Master is still looking for him. At supper this evening, Cook told Ruth and Miriam James's history. He's been here since he was ten years old. He is forty now.

Master's father gave James to Master and Mistress for a wedding present. That's why Master

was so close to James — giving him special privileges, like passes to go out, new clothing, and his
own room in The House. "He always been a favorite," Cook said.

Then she said that James went to North Carolina to look for his brothers and sisters. His mama
died when he was a boy. When I was sweeping in
the drawing room, I heard Mistress say to her husband, "How could he leave us without even saying
good-bye? He is not to ever come back here. He is
not to come near this house," she cried. "He's nothing but lazy trash, just like the rest of them."

I never thought I'd hear Mistress talk about
James like that. I never speak to Mistress unless
she speaks to me, so I didn't tell her that he went to
North Carolina to find his kin. It wasn't none of my
business to tell no how.

Friend, even though James never said much to
me, he was never cruel to me. I suppose his back
was so straight and his head so high he just never
saw little Patsy limping underfoot. He was more of
a gentleman than Master was, for I never heard
James yell or cuss. I don't think it was nice of Mistress to call him lazy trash. And who is "the rest of
them?" I wonder.

Next time someone gives Master and Mistress a
present, they ought to make sure that it can't walk

away. I hope that James finds his family. I wish I had a family to find, then perhaps I would find a name as well.

Sunday, April 30, 1865

Dear Friend,

Mistress and Sarah went to church today. Master stayed home and kept to the library. I think he is still grieving over James.

Nancy was fit to be tied because she had to remain at home and look after the children. Mistress told Nancy that she was responsible for both children. She told me to help.

The little girl, Nellie, is only a few months old and no trouble. She just wants to be held and rocked. But the boy, Thomas, is two years old and like a little hurricane. Nancy has to run behind him. It makes me grateful to have a limp, otherwise I would have to mind the more difficult child.

I sat on the bench under the leaning oak. I call it that because the trunk bends almost to the ground and the branches curve upward. Since James is gone, Mister Joe drove Sarah and Mistress to church in the carriage. Mister Joe is the only free black person I knew during slavery. He had to carry a paper on him showing that he was free, along with letters from the people he worked for saying that he was a right kind of honest man. Does he still carry those papers on him? I wonder.

Mister Joe lives near Davis Hall and hires himself out to Master and the other farmers in the neighborhood. Cook calls him Mister Anything because he does any kind of work. This morning, Mister Joe is the coachman.

As I rocked Nellie, I could hear, faintly, the hands singing in the arbor. In St. Philip's Church we have to sit upstairs in the slave gallery, and near the end of the service Father Holmes looks up at us and tells us that we must be good slaves and listen to our masters just as we listen to our Master in heaven.

Father Holmes would say the catechism. He asked the questions and we had to answer. I know it by heart because he says it every Sunday. It goes like this.

Question:	Who keeps the snakes and all bad things from hurting you?
Answer:	God does.
Question:	Who gave you a master and a mistress?

Answer:	God gave them to me.
Question:	Who says that you must obey them?
Answer:	God says that I must.
Question:	What book tells you these things?
Answer:	The Bible.
Question:	How does God do all his work?
Answer:	He always does it right.
Question:	Does God have to work?
Answer:	Yes, God is always at work.
Question:	Do the angels work?
Answer:	Yes, they do what God tells them.
Question:	Do they love to work?
Answer:	Yes, they love to please God.
Question:	What does God say about your work?
Answer:	He that does not work, does not eat.
Question:	Did Adam and Eve have to work?
Answer:	Yes, they had to keep the garden.
Question:	Was it hard to keep that garden?
Answer:	No, it was very easy.
Question:	What makes the crops so hard to grow now?
Answer:	Sin makes it.
Question:	What makes you lazy?
Answer:	My wicked heart.
Question:	How do you know your heart is wicked?
Answer:	I feel it every day.

Question:	Who teaches you so many wicked things?
Answer:	The Devil.
Question:	Must you let the Devil teach you?
Answer:	No, I must not.

These words were only for us up in the gallery. The white people didn't have to say them. Maybe Father Holmes had another catechism he used for them when we weren't around. Didn't the Yankee tell Father Holmes we was free? He said the same catechism last Sunday. One day I will read a Bible for myself and see if it says those things. My heart is not wicked.

Friend, I want to sit in the library, too, as Master does. I could easily hold Nellie and read a book at the same time. Instead, I rocked Nellie and listened to the beautiful singing from the bush arbor. I imagined that a gentle breeze carried the people's voices to the leaning oak, just for me to hear.

Dear Friend,

James is not the only one who has left Davis Hall Plantation. Today, while Mistress and Sarah visited with friends, and Nancy and I minded the children, two young men strolled down the walkway toward the gate.

The overseer ran behind them, yelling for them to come back and shouting that they cannot break the work contract.

Master rushed out of The House to see what the commotion was about. "Can't you control the hands?" he shouted at the overseer.

"If I can't whip them anymore, then I can't control them," the overseer answered angrily.

When I watched them walk away, my heart felt heavy. I wanted to limp behind them. Maybe they were going to find their families. Maybe I had a mother and a father, or a sister and a brother somewhere to find as well. But, Friend, where would I even start to look?

Tuesday, May 2, 1865

Dear Friend,

I must make more candles, otherwise I won't be able to write to you when it is dark. Three more field hands left today. At first I thought that one of them was Douglass. It wasn't. I did recognize a boy named Richard, who is about Douglass's age and used to work with the cobbler. The overseer flew into a rage.

Master saw them leave, too, for he ran out of The House. But the men kept walking, ignoring them both. The overseer threatened to arrest them, beat them, and all manner of terrible things. Said he was going to get the Yankees to gag them, hang them by the thumbs, and then shoot them. Master quieted him down as they both watched the men walk down the path that led them away from Davis Hall, just as the men had done the day before.

This evening, as we ate our supper, Ruth said she heard that rich Yankees were buying land and paying good wages and perhaps the hands were going to work on one of those farms. She also talked about James and about the many people who were searching for relatives.

All of this talk made me think about my own

history. Cook is the oldest and has always lived on Davis Hall. Maybe she knew my mother or father, or if I had sisters and brothers. I tried to find the courage to ask her, but she talked so much and so fast that I couldn't get a word in.

If we're free, my Friend, then we ought to be able to come and go as we please. Suppose everyone leaves because they all have family to search for. Who do I have to find? Will I be left by my own self at Davis Hall? Still living like a slave?

Wednesday, May 3, 1865

Dear Friend,

Each day brings something new. As I was lighting the cooking fire this morning, I saw all of the men and women who work the fields walk up to The House. "What happen now?" Cook mumbled. She told me to start kneading the biscuit dough, then she left.

I wanted to know what was happening also, but had to wait until noon when Miriam came to the kitchen to gossip with Cook. The field hands demanded that Master get rid of the overseer and let them pick their own boss from among themselves, otherwise they'd leave, too. When Master reminded them that they'd signed a contract, one of the women said she'd tear it up and then there would be no contract.

Cook said, "You know that slender handsome fellow, name Douglass? The one who ask the Yankee if we was free? He speak for everyone. He say, 'Sir, if we leave, you won't bring in no cotton crop, and you won't have no corn or potatoes. We still find work, but you can't find seventy-six experienced, hardworking hands like us this time of year.'"

Douglass is so brave. I am ashamed of myself at times, my Friend, for I cannot even speak up to the people I am with everyday.

I did not see the overseer later that afternoon, and the hands worked the fields as always. Master must have fired him like the hands demanded. Who is the boss now? I wonder.

There was no time to make the candles today either. When I wasn't holding Nellie I had to help Cook. I didn't even have time to think about my name. My Friend, maybe tomorrow I will tell Master that unless he lets me read for a spell every day, I will leave Davis Hall, too. Are you laughing, Friend? I am. Master would probably give me a kick in my hind parts and say good riddance. Then where would I be?

Dear Friend,

Nellie is sleeping and Cook is gossipping with Ruth. I snuck away for a moment to tell you this. When I was coming back from the dairy with milk this morning, a man at the gate called me. "Say, little girl, Miriam live here?"

I nodded my head.

"I'm her mother's brother," the man said. "Is she here right now?"

"Yes," I stammered out, but he dashed away from the gate and ran down the path toward the woods behind the cabins before I had a chance to say that Miriam was in The House ironing.

Later on, as I was washing the breakfast plates, I saw Miriam hurrying toward the gate, with her laundry basket on her head. I thought she was carrying Doctor Ashley's wash to him since Miriam does Doctor Ashley's laundry, too, but Master gets the money that the doctor pays.

Then, just before noon, Mistress came storming down the passageway toward the kitchen shed. "I can't find Miriam anywhere. Where is she?" Miriam always took her time coming back from Doctor Ashley, but it had been a while since I'd seen her. I knew then that she's not returning. She is with her mother's brother. I tried to tell Cook.

"Gal, hush that stammering and tend to your own business."

I know it's not a nice thing to say, but it will be our secret, Friend: At times I hate Cook.

Friday, May 5, 1865

Dear Friend,

It rained so hard today, but when it stopped the sun was bright and the air smelled fresh and clean.

When Nancy entered the kitchen this afternoon to take some tea to Mistress and Sarah, she told Cook and Ruth that Master and Mistress are sad because everyone is leaving. Cook sucked her teeth so loud, it echoed from the kitchen to the road. Cook said, "They sad because slavery is over and we all is equal now." Then she put her hands on her hips and said, "Nancy, I been meaning to tell you. Stop saying Master and Mistress. That's slavery-time talk. Sir and Ma'am be good enough."

Ruth agreed and added that she could also say Mister Davis and Missus Davis.

"You ain't my mistress," Nancy said, as she

always did whenever Cook scolded her. Then Cook threatened to slap the daylights out of her and Nancy picked up the tea tray and left in a huff. It's a good thing Cook can't read my mind or my writing, because I still say Master and Mistress, too. It sounds mighty strange to say anything else. But Cook is right and I will try to call them Mister Davis and Missus Davis. Or maybe I will simply call them Ma'am and Sir. Most times I don't say anything directly to them no how.

I need to think more about what to call my own self.

Saturday, May 6, 1865

Dear Friend,

Mistress, I mean to say Ma'am, informed Cook that if Miriam returned she would be arrested. "She owes us for the food, clothes, and lodging we have given her." All Cook said was, "Yes, Ma'am."

I'm wondering how could your slave work if she has no food and no place to sleep? Wasn't Ma'am and Sir supposed to feed Miriam and the rest of us?

I have to do the laundry now that Miriam is gone. I hope I don't have to do Doctor Ashley's wash, too, but if I do shouldn't I get to keep the money for myself since I'm supposed to be free? I heard James say once that Doctor Ashley pays Sir eight dollars a month for Miriam to do his laundry.

I make so many trips to the well to carry the water to the kitchen shed. Then I throw the water in the washpot and heat it on the coals. Ma'am complains that I am too slow. I heard Ruth say to Cook, "That child is too lame and small for such a big job." So in between her own cleaning, Ruth helps me carry water from the well to The House, and Luke helps me hang the clothes on the fence behind the kitchen shed.

I'd rather watch Nellie, but her own mother must do that when I have to do laundry. Nancy still watches the Wild One who darts about like a little white streak. Cook says he needs an old-fashioned, slavery-time spanking.

I will be so happy when we finally have a school here, so I can read and write all day long.

Sunday, May 7, 1865

Dear Friend,

It's a good thing that God made Sundays, otherwise I would hardly have time to talk to you. After

Ruth and I served breakfast, the family, even Master, I mean to say Sir, went to church. St. Philip's isn't far from here, so me, Nancy, and Miriam always walk. Only the family rides in the carriage. But I didn't want to go with them today even though I'd put on my other homespun dress, which I washed and ironed, and my blue Sunday kerchief. I stayed in the storeroom until everyone left. Ma'am wouldn't miss me.

Since I'm free, I ought to be able to do as I wish on Sundays. Ma'am might find some dusting for me to do in God's house if I go to church with her. I took off my Sunday clothes and put on my old dress and kerchief and got a dust rag out of the rag box.

No one was in The House, and Cook and Ruth had gone to the bush arbor. I took myself and my dust rag to the library to find my favorite book, *Little Goody Two-Shoes.*

Friend, you will never suppose what happened. I found the book, sat on the floor, and lost my whole self in the story.

"What're you doing in here?" I looked up and Ma'am and Nancy were standing over me.

"D-d-d, dusting," I sputtered, making myself look confused while wiping the book furiously.

"Don't you know it's Sunday? Patsy, you're

becoming more foolish each day. Leave those books alone. Don't dust them unless I tell you to."

I decided to play the dunce and tell Ma'am I thought it was Saturday.

She didn't let me finish. She just said to help Nancy make tea and then help Cook with supper.

Nancy walked alongside me, giggling. She said I looked like a dimwit, sitting on the floor, making believe I was reading. If I didn't have so much trouble with saying words, I would have told her that my wits could never be as dim as hers.

While we ate supper this evening, Cook and Ruth talked about Miriam, after Nancy left the table. Cook said that Miriam's mother had planned all along for Miriam to go with her as soon as the War was over. She lived on Sir's plantation on Edisto Island. I wonder where Miriam and her mother will live now. You know, Friend, maybe my mother will come for me. That thought makes me feel happy.

Now I have to be careful. I do not want anyone to know that I can read and write. Something inside of me tells me that I should keep it a secret for a while longer. Maybe it is still illegal. Maybe I'm not supposed to know how until I go to school.

Monday, May 8, 1865

Dear Friend,

I cannot remain long for I am so tired. Ma'am tried to show me how to iron, but she doesn't know how herself. I smudged all of Sir's shirts with the pieces of coal left on the bottom of the iron, and she called me stupid.

I work with three irons, two on the coals and one to press with. When the one I'm pressing with cools down, then I take one of the irons off the coals and use that. But I was so afraid of burning his shirts I didn't let the iron get hot enough. I have hidden the half-ironed shirts in the bottom of one of the laundry baskets. Tomorrow I will try to do better.

Tuesday, May 9, 1865

Dear Friend,

Ruth helped me iron today, so I had time to make some candles. Cook gave me some beef fat. I boil the fat and put the candle molds in cold water in a tin tub. Then I put a string down the middle of the mold and pour the hot fat over it. Once the fat is hard and has shrunk from the cold water, it drops away from the mold without breaking up in pieces and you have a perfect candle. Cook said, "You do know how to make a candle." I think that's the only thing I know how to do good. If Ruth hadn't helped me with the ironing, I never would have finished.

Now I can write to you all night. If only I had the *Little Goody Two-Shoes* book, then I could read all night, too.

Wednesday, May 10, 1865

What excitement this morning! I was in the kitchen cleaning the ashes out of the fireplace when Cook and I heard Nancy screaming and yelling from the front yard. Cook ran out of the kitchen and I limped behind her. Nancy held on to Ma'am so tight, I thought she'd tear Ma'am's skirt binding loose. A small, brown woman stood in front of them. Something about her looked familiar. She wore a pink gingham dress. Her thick hair was braided in one long plait wound around her head. The woman reached for Nancy, but Nancy backed away, clinging even tighter to Ma'am.

"You cannot take her!" Ma'am shouted at the woman. "She belongs here."

"I am her mother," the woman shouted back.

Ma'am turned so red, I thought flames would shoot out of her head. She told the woman that she had raised Nancy and given her a good home.

"You raised her to be your slave. Slavery done. She don't belong to you no more." She hurled her words like stones in Ma'am's face.

Then Nancy cried, "I don't know you."

The woman spoke to Nancy. "You was only four years old when she took you from me, and I begged her to let me keep you. I am your mother." Nancy kept sobbing and holding on to Ma'am.

Before Ma'am could say anything, Sir rushed out of the house and ordered the woman to leave. She refused.

The blood rose up in Sir's face. He said that legally, they could keep Nancy because she is their apprentice and must stay with them until she is eighteen years of age. Then he ordered her to leave his property or he'd have her arrested for trespassing and vagrancy.

Sir, Ma'am, and Nancy walked up the stairs to The House. Ma'am put her arms around Nancy. The sobbing woman screamed after them, "She is my child and I mean to take her with me." She wiped her eyes with the back of her hands and, holding herself straight, walked slowly to the gate and stepped outside of it. She faced The House and stood as though her feet had grown roots. I glanced back at her before I limped back to the kitchen, and suddenly I realized why she seemed familiar. Nancy looked just like her. I felt so sorry for the woman and will never forget her face, wet with tears, and her lonely eyes.

Friend, every time I went outside after that, I saw Nancy's mother standing, staring — it worried me so. I didn't see Nancy for the rest of the morning — even when I went into The House to help Ruth clean. Ruth made the bed in Ma'am's chamber and I put fresh water in the pitcher. I peeped out of the window. Nancy's mother was still there. I called Ruth and pointed. "Oh, Lord, that poor soul's still standing at the gate. I thought she left."

Friend, I found the courage to ask whether Nancy's mother could stay in my room.

Ruth shook her head and said she had another idea. She left the chamber and told me to continue my chores. When I went outside to empty the chamber pots, the woman was gone. What did Ruth do?

I don't understand Nancy. How happy I would be to have a mother of my own to come and look for me.

Dear Friend,

I found out where Nancy's mother is. Ruth asked one of the families in the quarters to take her in. Nancy is a foolish girl. People think I am a dimwit, but Nancy is the dunce. When she came into the kitchen to eat her supper, her mouth was full of twaddle, and her tears were dry. "Mistress say that the woman can't take me away because I am a minor," she declared to Ruth and Cook.

I saw the way Cook and Ruth glanced at one another. I don't think they liked what Nancy said. Then Cook told Nancy, "If she your mother, you must go with her."

Friend, why did Cook say that? Nancy's tears rose up like a river flooding its banks. She cried that Mistress say the people who leave their good masters are starving on the roads. The Yankees give them stick-and-mud houses to live in like the poor whites have. And the Yankees are selling black people to a far country called Cuba, where they are slaves. "I'll starve to death if I go with her. I'll have no more clean white, starched aprons."

I kept eating and made believe I didn't even hear Nancy's talk. Cook sucked her teeth so loud, it made me and Luke jump. "She filling your empty head with lies, fool," was all Cook said. Nancy was sorely insulted and left the kitchen and half her stew. Ruth put some of the food in Luke's plate and the rest in mine. Then she patted me on the shoulder and told Cook that I gave her the idea to help Nancy's mother. Cook said, "Patsy don't give no trouble. Just a bit slowful." I think Cook was trying to give me a compliment, but I don't like it when people talk about me as if I am not even in the room.

I learned more about Nancy's mother. Her name is Mary Ella, and when Nancy was taken away from her to live in The House, Mary Ella made such a fuss, Sir sent her to work on his other plantation on Edisto Island.

Cook said that Nancy was a beautiful little girl. Ma'am had recently lost a baby girl in childbirth when she took Nancy to raise in The House. Ma'am has no children of her own.

Their talk made me wonder again about my own history. Did Ma'am take me away from my mother, too? I don't suppose I was such a beautiful baby though. I tried to ask Cook who my mother is.

"What you worrying yourself for? Nobody going to take you away," was all she said.

Friend, Cook didn't say to hush up, but that's what she meant for me to do. She took my meaning all wrong. After that, I didn't feel like asking any more questions.

Mary Ella will leave Davis Hall tomorrow, but she plans to go to the magistrate and try to get Nancy back.

Friend, why does an ungrateful girl like Nancy have a mother to come for her and I do not?

Friday, May 12, 1865

Dear Friend,

I wonder when Miss Mary Ella will return for Nancy. If I have a mother and she comes for me, I will not treat her the way Nancy treats her own mother. I will tell her how much I love her and miss her.

My Friend, suddenly I am anxious. What will happen if someone comes for me? I've never lived anywhere else but here at Davis Hall. How would it feel to live somewhere else? I wonder. Are people dying on the roads and starving like Ma'am says?

Maybe that's why Nancy is afraid to go with her mother. Still, if my mother or father or anybody comes to claim me, I will go. For I know I mean no more to Ma'am and Sir than the other objects they own. The only difference with me is that I can walk and talk, and not so good at that either.

Sunday, May 14, 1865
Morning

Dear Friend,

I thought that the Lord's Day would never come. I have not had one moment alone to write to you. Everyone except Sir is going to church — even the baby. Mister Joe is waiting outside the gate with the carriage. I am hiding here in my chamber (storeroom) as I did last Sunday, until everyone is gone.

Sir remains in the library so I cannot go in there. I have decided to worship in the bush arbor with Ruth, Cook, and the field hands. Maybe I am not free to leave the plantation, but I am free to go to the bush arbor. Will Ruth and Cook think it strange to see me there? I wonder.

I will write to you this evening and tell you what the arbor is like. I hope Douglass is there.

Evening

The world has gone crazy. Cook is leaving and everything is a mess. I must go to help Ruth serve the family their dinner.

Monday, May 15, 1865

Dear Friend,

It is so strange now without Cook. I wondered yesterday why she didn't go to the bush arbor as she usually did on Sundays. I couldn't go either because she told me to cut up the meat for pepper pot stew. When Ma'am and Sir came from church, Cook went to The House. I knew something was wrong. Cook rarely went to The House.

A few moments later, she returned to the kitchen shed. Ma'am and Sir, looking upset, rushed in after her.

I've never seen Ma'am so begging. I was surprised that she didn't fly into one of her red rages. Her voice cracked as she spoke. She said, "You have been the best of servants. My mother depended upon you, and you made her last days comfortable. We all relied on you when anyone was ill. You nursed me through four confinements. Please,

Susan, don't leave us." (Susan is Cook's real name.)

Sir told Cook that he would pay her twice what her new employers were going to give her. Cook refused. "If I stay in this house where I been a slave, I'll never know I'm free. This here stew I made should last a couple of days till you get another cook." She turned around and, without another word or a smile, walked away from the kitchen shed with a small bundle of her belongings balanced on her head.

I limped across the lawn behind her. It was my last chance to ask her about my history. I tried mightily not to stammer as I called to her.

She frowned. "Come on, gal. Stop hooting like a owl. Say what you want to say."

I finally got it out. But she doesn't know who my mother is. She said I came here with a new passel of slaves Sir bought. There was only men in the bunch and me. One of the men was holding me. She didn't think he was my pa, and she said my mother probably died somewhere along the way. Ma'am brought me to The House and Cook brought me back from near death. Then one of the old women in the quarters kept me, but I took sick again and Ma'am carried me back to The House. I been there ever since. That's all she knew.

"Patsy, now you forget about all them old slavery-time things what happened. It done."

She opened the gate and took one last look at The House. I waved good-bye to her, and she waved back and smiled. I think that was the first time she ever smiled at me.

My heart is sad, thinking of a mother who may have died.

As I sit here writing in the storeroom, I can't help thinking about Cook. It doesn't feel right in the kitchen without her looking miserable and saying something comical about everyone. I wish I knew all along that Cook had taken care of me when I was a sick baby. I am sorry that I hated her sometimes and thought she was mean. She was just being Cook.

Will I have to leave in order to be truly free, like Cook says? Friend, is my mother in heaven watching over me? Maybe she and God will protect me if I leave Davis Hall, too.

Tuesday, May 16, 1865
Sunrise

Dear Friend,

I will not be able to stay long. The wake-up horn has blown and I must help Ruth. She is cooking and cleaning now. When I am not washing and ironing I help her. Nancy is supposed to help also. Ma'am wants Ruth to show Nancy how to cook.

Ruth said to me, "That Nancy don't want to do nothing but follow behind Missus Davis and Sarah." When Ruth tried to show Nancy how to knead the biscuit dough, Nancy told Ruth that Mistress was training her to be a fine ladies' maid, not a cook. I thought Ruth would throw the skillet at Nancy's head.

I didn't think I could miss Cook so much.

One more thing, Nancy had the nerve to say that I don't get the clothes as clean as Miriam did.

I stammered out for her to clean them herself. She left the kitchen before I finished my sentence. I was glad I spoke up anyhow, even if she didn't hear all of it.

Wednesday, May 17, 1865

Dear Friend,

Green sprouts dot the cotton, corn, and potato fields. The best thing that happened today was that Nancy got a spanking. Ruth had to clean in The House this morning so Nancy had to make the biscuits. Ma'am came in the kitchen to make sure

Nancy was kneading the dough properly. When did Ma'am learn how to knead dough? I wonder.

I had to lower my face so Nancy wouldn't see me laughing at those hard lumpy biscuits she made. I knew Sir would have a fit. One bite and he almost broke a tooth. He told Ma'am, "You can't show these girls how to make a decent biscuit?"

Ma'am couldn't hold her sharp tongue. "I was raised to be a lady, not a cook." She told him to hire a cook from among the field hands and he shouted that he couldn't spare any of them. "The only thing between us and poverty are them field hands," he thundered. Made me jump, too, and he wasn't even fussing at me. Ma'am got so angry, she cussed Yankees and black people and gave Nancy a spanking.

I bet Nancy wishes now that she'd paid some mind when Ruth was showing her how to knead dough, and I bet she wishes she'd left with her own mother.

Thursday, May 18, 1865

Dear Friend,

I am dead tired. I spent the entire day ironing because I had to do Sir's shirts over again. He said they were wrinkled. But I was able to dust in the library and snuck a peek at *Goody Two-Shoes*. I love the part where she teaches herself how to read and then teaches all of the children in the countryside as well.

Friday, May 19, 1865

Dear Friend,

There was a soft, sweet, quiet rain all day. Such a new thing occurred. I saw many of the field hands walk across the lawn in the direction of the gate instead of working until sunset as they always did. None of the children or the very old people were with them. I tapped Ruth and pointed at the group. I thought they were all leaving. I looked to see whether Douglass was among them, but he wasn't.

Ruth stopped hanging the pots over the fireplace and stepped out of the shed. She smiled, and her deep dimples made her look so very pretty. "They going to the magistrate to get a legal marriage. No more of them slavery-time marriages that don't mean nothing." She folded her arms the way she always did when she and Cook gossiped. "They be back."

Ruth likes to talk and now she has only me.

Friend, it felt real nice to have her talk to me in just the same way she used to gossip with Cook and Miriam.

Luke ran across the passageway from The House to the kitchen. His little round face was lit up like a lantern as he held out his hand. "Look, Mama, Mister Davis Sir give me a nickel for polishing all the shoes." Then he turned to show me, his hand open and the shiny coin in the middle of his palm.

He gave his mother the money and told her to buy something nice for herself when they go to the store. Then he ran past the stables toward the cabins where he has other children to play with. I finished sweeping, and we both sat down at the kitchen table and waited for the married couples to return. I felt close enough to Ruth to ask where Luke's Daddy is. Her dimples and smile disappeared when she told me this story:

Luke's father freed himself. He ran away from Davis Hall when the War began. He heard that the Yankees was freeing folks. Ruth wanted to go with him, but he said it was too dangerous, especially for Luke who was a baby.

He begged Ruth to wait here for him. But now she doesn't know if he is dead or alive. She said she would've left with Cook if she knew for sure John wasn't coming back. All she wants is for her and John to have a real marriage and for Luke to go to school.

"We still living like slaves here," she said.

Friend, her words made me feel so very sad. I hope Luke's father didn't die in the War. But I don't want Luke and Ruth to leave. She is becoming like an older sister, and Luke is like having a little brother. Maybe when the school comes to Davis Hall, Ruth will stay.

The only thing that makes me happy, Friend, is that Douglass wasn't among those couples getting married. Will anyone ever want to marry me? I wonder.

Saturday, May 20, 1865

Dear Friend,

I am tired. Ruth and I are working so hard. Nancy never helps us. She always complains that she is too busy with caring for the children, or that she has to comb Ma'am's hair, or Sarah's hair.

I am glad Ruth hasn't said anything about leaving Davis Hall. Luke chattered all day long about the things he will buy at the store. I am sure he's spent at least five hundred dollars already.

Dear Friend,

Finally, I made it to the bush arbor! I will tell you all about it, Friend. Word for word, as I remember. By the time I reached the pond, I heard people singing, "Oh, blow your trumpet, Gabriel, blow your trumpet louder." And when I reached the cypress grove I saw everyone sitting on logs and on the ground around a clearing. They'd created a great arbor with leaves, branches, and vines.

I was glad no one seemed to notice me as I sat down on the ground. Ruth and Luke didn't see me. Douglass was sitting next to his mother and a young woman. I hope she is his sister.

Brother Solomon was leading the singing. When they finished he said, "This is a blessed day," and congratulated all of the couples who had married on Friday. Then he said, "Me and my Violet have been together for twenty years. By the grace of God we was never sold away from each other, or our children. And by the grace of God we is now married like all free peoples in this here country."

"Amens" drowned out the birds. And then Brother Solomon shouted, "We are free at last."

Violet, short and round, added her words. "I thank God I'm free at last."

"On this bright morning, I thank God I'm free at last," Ruth sang out and began to clap.

Mother Naomi, leaning on her walking stick, stood up, and her words came out of her mouth with a melody. "Way down yonder in the graveyard walk," and everyone repeated, "Free at last."

Then Douglass sang out, "On my knees when the light passed by," and everyone repeated, "Free at last. I thank God I'm free at last."

Douglass sang out again. "Thought my soul would rise and fly."

Everyone repeated, "Free at last. I thank God I'm free at last."

I didn't feel as if I were on Davis Hall Plantation anymore. The bush arbor, the quarters, the prayers and songs made this seem like a place apart. Friend, I thought my soul would rise and fly, too.

Douglass stepped forward and said a prayer thanking God for helping us gain our freedom and then he thanked God for Brother Solomon, "Our new boss."

Everyone said, "Amen."

Then Violet stood up and spoke to the people. I guess God heard her, too. "Thanks be to God we no longer slaves. Now we will get money for the cotton we grow. And thanks be to God we ain't got no trash with a whip trying to sap our last bit of strength. We have our own Brother Solomon and lord knows Solomon can bring in a cotton crop. He been planting cotton longer than some of us been living . . ."

Someone shouted, "All right, Sister Violet, come to the point."

"The point is we are not so free yet. We need land of our own. We still depending on our use-to-be Master. It's his cottonseed we planting, it's his cabins we still living in, and it's his land. We need land of our own — then we free!"

"And we need a school for these children," Ruth added.

Brother Solomon said, "We only been free a month. We need a lot of things, but we own our own selves now, and we will find a way to get everything we want."

How different from St. Philip's Church! There, no one talks but Father Holmes and people only sing the hymns written down in the books. Nobody makes up a song from their hearts together, like "Free at Last." And in the arbor there was no catechism about us being wicked.

Ruth seemed happy and surprised when she finally saw me. "Patsy, I'm glad you come here to worship with us," she said.

Friend, I don't know why, but I felt free in the bush arbor.

Unfortunately, my good feelings disappeared as soon as I had to serve Ma'am her afternoon tea. When I placed the teacup and saucer on her table, she said, "By the way, Patsy, you haven't been to church for three Sundays. I will not have an ungodly, wicked child in this house. You can't be so dim-witted that you have to be told it's Sunday and time for church when you see everyone else going?"

Friend, I closed my eyes and thought of the bush arbor, and "Free at Last," and I found the courage to tell her I went to the arbor.

She called it foolishness and told me to make sure I was in St. Philip's next Sunday. But I will not go. I am not a baby, and I am not wicked or ungodly. Friend, I mean to keep going to the arbor, no matter what. By the way, Friend, the girl sitting next to Douglass this morning is his sister.

Monday, May 22, 1865

Dear Friend,

Ruth didn't feel well this morning. Ma'am told Nancy to make the breakfast biscuits. I saw the way she was kneading the dough and not putting in enough milk and I knew they'd be some rock-hard biscuits again, and she'd get another spanking. I knew exactly how to make biscuits, because Cook showed me. But I suppose Ma'am thought I was too dim-witted to do it.

I had to wash anyway and was having enough trouble with that. But as I dumped the clothes in the washpot I felt sorry for Nancy and showed her how to get the dough just right.

"How do you know?" she asked. I didn't even answer her. Let her get another whipping. "If these biscuits ain't right, I'll tell Master you told me to do it this way."

The biscuits came out just right. Nancy rushed into the dining room and then came back with all of her teeth showing, telling me how everyone was licking up those biscuits.

Seems to me that she forgot who told her how to get it right.

Tuesday, May 23, 1865

Dear Friend,

Ruth still doesn't feel too well, so I told her that I'd do all of the cleaning after we served breakfast.

She thanked me and told Luke to help me when I began the ironing. Luke folded the clothes and made sure that the irons stayed hot. As soon as the iron I was using cooled down he handed me one of the irons that was still on the hot coals.

Ma'am complained about everything — especially the way I cleaned — and yelled at Ruth for not taking care of the cleaning herself. "You know Patsy can't do anything right!"

Ruth surprised me. She never used to sass Ma'am. But she said, "Patsy's doing the best she can, and she is a big help."

Ma'am turned red, but all she said was, "I'll get Nancy to help Patsy." I hate working with Nancy. Ma'am stayed behind us to make sure everything was done the way Ruth did it. She even yelled at her pet, Nancy.

Friend, I admire the way Ruth spoke up. I want to try to be more like her.

Ma'am worries me to death. "You had better try harder, Patsy. How can I continue to care for you?" What if she makes me leave? Where will I go? I pray every day that there will be someone at the gate for me.

Thursday, May 25, 1865

Dear Friend,

I have another history to tell. Mister Joe's. Ruth told it to me this morning. He doesn't have a wife anymore. She died. She wasn't free like him. He was trying to save up enough money to buy her freedom, but she was with child before Mister Joe could buy her. The baby didn't belong to Mister Joe and his wife because, under the slave law, if a woman had a baby, that baby was the possession of the master who owned the woman.

Mister Joe's marriage was no more real than any other slave marriage, even though Mister Joe was free. His wife's master let her be with Mister Joe, but she was still the cook for the family, and she was still a slave.

When I asked about the baby, Ruth lowered her voice so that I could hardly hear her.

"Patsy, don't you never tell this." This is what she told me. I know you can keep the secret, Friend. Mister Joe's wife never let her master know she was with child. She made believe she was just gaining weight. And when it was time for the baby to be born, Mister Joe came for Cook who delivered a baby girl.

Mister Joe carried the baby to Charleston for his sister to keep, until he could buy his wife's freedom. But his wife died before he could save enough money to buy her. Mister Joe's sister is raising the girl, and she is being educated in a private school for free black children in Charleston.

That's why he stays here working so hard. He's paying for his daughter's education. He gets more work from these farmers than he could get in Charleston doing his barber trade. His daughter has never come here because under slave law she belonged to her mother's master. It made me angry that Mister Joe wasn't allowed to keep his own daughter. But all that is over now. Will she come to visit? I wonder.

Friend, I had to tell you Mister Joe's history because it makes me feel strong to write about brave people like Mister Joe and his wife and Cook. They could've been whipped and jailed for what they did. But they wouldn't let anyone rule them. I will try to be like them. I feel sorry for every bad thought I ever had about Cook.

Dear Friend,

Mister Joe ate with us again this evening, and I was glad. After supper, Ruth and I were cleaning the dishes, and I heard Mister Joe tell Luke a wonderful story. He said his mother had told it to him and her mother had told it to her. Now I will tell it to you.

Once upon a time in Africa there was people who knew how to fly. Magic men showed them. One day, some of those same Africans was captured and stuffed into slave ships. They took sick and their great black wings wilted like dead flowers. The white men who'd stolen them didn't see the people's dying wings.

The people kept their magic secret when they reached a plantation right here in South Carolina. And one day, years later, when the heat was unbearable and the overseer's whip bit into their legs and backs, an old man who remembered, spoke the magic words.

The people gathered strength from his words. They repeated them and felt a pulling and a wrenching on their backs as their dead wings sprouted to life. Such a flapping and a swooshing you never did hear as the people got their power back. One by one, they raised their arms and flew away from the fields and the overseer's whip. They flew right back to their homes in Africa.

I love this story and am writing it down so that I will always remember it. Ruth laughed at it though. Said that Mister Joe needs to stop telling those slavery-time stories. "We have our wings now, Mister Joe. We can fly away whenever we want to."

I wanted to say to her, Why are we still here then? I wish I could ask Mister Joe about his daughter and the school she goes to, but I am not supposed to know his secret.

Saturday, May 27, 1865

Dear Friend,

I think Ruth was wrong when she said we had our wings. Today a terrible thing happened. Douglass's friend Richard was brought back by a Yankee soldier, the same one who had first told us we were free. Sir called all of the hands out of the fields to the front lawn. Ruth and I went also.

The soldier said that a contract must be honored and could not be broken. Then he turned to Richard and said if he tried to break the contract again he would be put on a chain gang and made to work for nothing. Douglass put his arms around Richard and spoke quietly to him.

Brother Solomon and the rest of the hands looked angry. I kept thinking that it was too bad the young man couldn't fly. Then Brother Solomon's wife, Violet, and some of the others reminded the soldier that a school was part of the contract, too.

The soldier said that a missionary society would be sending teachers to the various plantation schools and promised that Davis Hall would have a school.

Finally! We will have a school, and I will be able to read and write for all to see. Friend, I cannot write too much tonight for now I really must think up a suitable name for myself. I'll need it for school!

Sunday, May 28, 1865

Dear Friend,

You will not imagine what happened today. I went to the bush arbor again!

The family did not go to church because the Wild One was ill, and Sarah and Ma'am had to tend to him. I know they miss Cook because she'd have brewed one of her teas for him and he'd have been his wild self again.

Nancy was minding Nellie, and after I finished helping serve the family breakfast, Ruth and I — with Luke running ahead of us — walked to the arbor. I didn't sneak or even tell Ma'am that I was going there. I just went.

I am going to try to remember every word and tell it to you just how it happened.

Brother Solomon introduced a man I'd never seen before. "Sisters and brothers," he said, with a smile as wide as the front lawn. "This be a special morning. The Reverend Chaplain Henry McNeal, the first black chaplain in the United States Army, and now doing important work with the Freedmen's Bureau is here to . . ."

Violet said, "Let the man speak, then." People laughed. The Reverend Henry McNeal looked as tall and strong as one of the largest oaks in the woods behind us. He smiled only slightly and his face seemed as if it had been carved out of the rough bark of oak trees.

I had never before seen a black man dressed as he was. He wore a minister's white collar like Father Holmes, and his jacket, vest, and pants were of a fine broadcloth, not the rough homespun that we wear. His black shoes shone like the sun.

I had never before heard anyone speak like him either. Oh, the wonderful things he told us. And the words he used sounded like the words I've seen in books and newspapers. He doesn't talk the way we do.

He said we should not be ashamed because we had once been enslaved. He said there were black people who had done great things. And then he talked about his own life.

He has always been free, but he worked in the cotton fields, too. I suppose he had that same kind of freedom like Mister Joe had.

He said so many wonderful things, I cannot forget them. He spoke about the American flag and said, "Every star is against us, every stripe against us. We want power, and it can only come through organization."

He talked about white people like Sir and Ma'am, and he said we should not remain angry with them because the past is done. "Let us show we can be a people, respectable, virtuous, honest, and industrious, and soon their prejudice will melt away. And with God for our Father, we will all be brothers. I hold that we are a very great people."

God in His heaven must have heard the shout when Reverend McNeal finished. He raised his arms and I believe that the Reverend McNeal has the power to fly, that his powerful arms could turn into great black wings. He has the magic and can give it to us.

As soon as the Reverend McNeal finished his talk and left the arbor, Ruth, Violet, and the other women began to talk about cleaning the spinning house and filling the chinks in the walls with clay. Mister Joe and the other men said that they will make benches for the schoolroom.

Friend, I will help the women, too. We must have everything just right for the teacher, otherwise she might not stay. Ruth seems as happy as I am. She wants to go to the school as well!

Monday, May 29, 1865
Sunrise

Dear Friend,

The horn has not even blown yet, but I am already awake. The Reverend McNeal's words still sound in my ears. When will we begin to clean the spinning house, and when will the men make the benches? I wonder. If I am able to complete the wash early today, I will go to the spinning house myself and begin. The teacher will probably be here any day. We must be ready when she comes.

Tuesday, May 30, 1865

Dear Friend,

I didn't go to the spinning house. Ruth said that since everyone is so busy during the week, we would begin to clean on Saturday or Sunday.

Sir and Ma'am seemed very happy today, and Sarah wasn't crying about her land. As I served breakfast, I heard Sir say, "The government has canceled our war debt. They've given us an amnesty." I'm wondering what amnesty means.

Sir is beginning to look almost like his old self again. Mister Joe's been shaving him and cutting his hair. But I know that Sir misses James.

I heard some bad news today. Sir found out from another farmer about Reverend McNeal and his meetings with the freed people on the farms in the neighborhood. He told Brother Solomon that he doesn't want outsiders on his land. He doesn't know that the outsider has already been here.

Sir invited the hands to worship at St. Philip's. I don't think they will go, and I don't think anyone can stop Reverend McNeal from speaking.

Wednesday, May 31, 1865

Dear Friend,

My hands are raw from all of the washing, especially Nellie's dirty linens. It seems as if Sunday
will never come. I hope the Reverend McNeal returns.

Thursday, June 1, 1865

Dear Friend,

This morning, after Luke and I left the dairy, we
walked to the spinning house. We peeked in. There
is so much cleaning to do.

"It look nasty in there, Patsy."

I tried to answer, but couldn't help stammering.

"What's the matter, Patsy?" he said, tilting his
little head and looking up in my mouth. "Is the
word stuck?"

He always says that and it always makes me
laugh. He's only a child and doesn't mean any
harm.

"When's the teacher coming, Patsy?"

"Soon," I said, without stuttering!

Friday, June 2, 1865

Dear Friend,

The fields are green with young cotton plants and potato and corn plants. Each day I watch the road and wonder whether Nancy's mother, Mary Ella, will return, and whether anyone else will leave. I wonder when the teacher will arrive. What will she be like? I hope she is kind and patient like Charles and Annie's teacher was.

Saturday, June 3, 1865

Dear Friend,

Today I completed the ironing and then Luke and I picked peaches and ate almost as many as we picked. After supper, me and Ruth carried water into The House so that everyone could bathe. When we finished toting water for the family, we hauled water for ourselves so that we could take turns bathing in the tin tub in the storeroom. (Of course, you were well hidden under my pallet.) Ruth hung the old sheet we always used for privacy around one corner of the shed.

I have been in the storeroom all evening, but I

was finally able to read the one page I kept from the newspapers that Ma'am told me to throw away.

I like to read about the things you can buy like Reddings Russia Salve for the cure of burns, cuts, flesh wounds, boils, chilblains, blisters, bruises, warts, old sores, ringworm, and frostbitten parts. It reminds me of Cook and her teas.

I am glad that tomorrow is Sunday. Will the people go to St. Philip's? I wonder. I won't. And Ruth said that she won't go either. If there is no worship in the arbor, I will stay in the storeroom until everyone is gone and then I will go to The House and into Sir's library to read.

Sunday, June 4, 1865

Dear Friend,

I was happy when I saw Ma'am and the rest of the family, including Sir, climb into the carriage to go to church. I don't make believe I am going to St. Philip's anymore. I will worship as I please.

I will try to remember it all for you. When Ruth and I arrived at the arbor I was glad to see that no one accepted Sir's invitation to go to St. Philip's. Best of all, the Reverend McNeal was there. He gave us his magic words again. He tells us to be strong and fear only God and not our former masters and mistresses. "My life has been threatened for the work I do, but I will not let anyone stop me from doing God's work for God's people."

He seemed to look at each and every one of us. "You can do great things. You can get the land you desire and you can educate your children." He tapped his forehead. "All you need is the will and the determination." He tapped his forehead again. "The determination is here. It is the most powerful tool you have. God bless you."

Brother Solomon stood up like he had found his wings and began to sing "Free at Last." Everyone joined him.

After the service, people had a chance to speak. Ruth was the first one to stand up. "Reverend Sir," she said, "it's June, and they's still no school for these young ones."

The Reverend said he talked to the people at the Freedmen's Bureau and told them we need schools out here. He said that his own African Methodist Episcopal Church is looking for young men to send to school in Baltimore to train for the ministry.

"Amen," Douglass called out. Does the Reverend's church have a school for girls? I wonder.

Violet asked about land. Reverend McNeal said

that the freed men and women are getting land that the former slave owners abandoned on the sea islands and the coast when the Yankees captured the islands. I suppose that's how Miss Sarah's slaves got her land.

The Yankee General Sherman is granting land to the freed men and their families. But Reverend McNeal advised everyone to stay here for now and work out their contract. He said that the military government has given the freed people land, but the military can also take it away.

When Reverend McNeal left, Ruth and I joined Violet and the other women in the spinning house. Luke and the older children helped, too. Violet gave Luke and I straw brooms to sweep the dirt floor. Some of the women began daubing the chinks in the walls with clay. A couple of older girls began to wipe down the walls. I don't mind cleaning when it's for a school.

Douglass and Richard hauled in a tin tub full of water. As soon as the girls saw them their voices got higher and louder. I don't suppose Douglass saw me, with the way those girls flounced up in his face.

I enjoyed getting the room ready for the teacher though. I imagined myself in school, sitting on a bench and learning everything. By the time we finished, the room was sparkling clean. All that we needed was a desk for the teacher and benches for the students.

Even though Ruth is excited about the school, she says that she doesn't know how much longer she can stay at Davis Hall, waiting for John. She wants better wages so she can have her own little home.

"I don't care if it be a tiny cabin, long as it's mine."

I don't like to hear Ruth talking about leaving, so I forced myself to speak about going to school and tried mightily not to stammer. I became so excited the word "school" stuck in my mouth. Ruth had to pull it out for me. Then she smiled at me and told me that school mightn't be right for me, but she said that I do tasks good when someone shows me how. She said I was getting better at ironing. "You try to do your best."

Friend, I know Ruth means no harm, because she is my only friend besides you, but she thinks I'm a dunce, too.

I wonder what she'd say if I told her I could read and write. She'd probably think I was lying.

When we walked into the kitchen, Ruth let out a long sigh. She took the skillet off the fireplace, and I started the cooking fire. "Cook was right. As long as we stay here, we never free," Ruth said.

I know Ruth is not my mother and she has her own child to care about, but I will be lonely and miserable here if she and Luke leave. And how can I leave Davis Hall? Where would I go? How would I get there?

Monday, June 5, 1865

Dear Friend,

It rained all day and I ironed all day. Mister Joe ate dinner with us again. He says he thinks that some of the hands and their families will leave Davis Hall and go to the coast because they want land more than anything, and they say Sir already broke the contract. They are not taking the Reverend's advice. They say they can't wait till next year for land. And Richard left again.

This time he went through the woods, instead of walking out of the front gate for all to see. But the woods are dangerous. Mister Joe says Confederate soldiers returning from the War are starving, poor, and angry. They blame us for their problems. Some of them call themselves Regulators. They patrol the woods. They say they are keeping the neighborhood safe from the wild black men who have been set free. Black bodies are being found all the time — hanging from trees, drowned in the creeks. Mister Joe says these are some dangerous times.

Ruth asked what would happen to the families who were leaving. Would they be returned to the plantation or killed by the Regulators? But Mister Joe didn't have an answer.

Tonight I will pray for Richard's safety, and I will pray for the families who plan to leave. Maybe some of them have the magic and can fly away.

Wednesday, June 7, 1865

Dear Friend,

Last night Ruth asked me to stay in the cottage with Luke while she went to the cabins. The room seems larger since Cook and Miriam are gone. Two homespun dresses hang on one hook and Luke's Sunday homespun trousers hang on another. A large basket holding several patchwork quilts stands in the corner and a small milking stool sits by the fireplace.

Luke was lying on his pallet and, Friend, I wished I had a book and a real oil lamp so I could read. Maybe read him a story. My Friend, you know I don't stammer when I read.

Leaning on his elbow with his hand under his

chin, Luke looked up at me, his bright eyes dancing. He asked me whether the teacher would be here tomorrow. I told him I didn't know when exactly, but soon. He asked me to tell him a story like Mister Joe does. Then he said that his mother told him when he goes to school he will learn how to read book stories.

I closed my eyes and leaned against the wall. I could see every word of *Little Goody Two-Shoes* in my mind's eye. I began to say the words as I saw them. I tried mightily not to stammer.

"This is the history of Little Goody Two-Shoes, otherwise called Missus Margery Two-Shoes . . ."

I heard a tiny snort. Luke was fast asleep. Finally, I speak without stammering and no one hears me.

As I watched Luke sleeping peacefully and listened to his little snores, I suddenly wanted to wake him up and tell him, I'll show you how to read, Luke. I can teach you all of your letters. And perhaps then Ruth won't want to leave Davis Hall.

You see, Friend, I keep wondering why Ruth went to the cabins last night. I worry that she's making plans to leave. I have to tell her my secret.

Thursday, June 8, 1865

Dear Friend,

When Mister Joe stopped by the kitchen for his morning glass of milk, he told Ruth about the meeting of the Union League next Tuesday. What is a Union League? I wonder. A church? And why are they meeting? Are they making plans to leave? I don't know what it all means. There are times when I am so very frightened because everything is changing, yet I am still Patsy who belongs to Ma'am and Sir.

Lately, I don't feel like Patsy, though. Inside I am beginning to feel like Ruth and Cook and Mister Joe, who do what their minds tell them to do.

Friday, June 9, 1865

Dear Friend,

What excitement today! Ma'am got a letter from the magistrate ordering her to appear before him, regarding Nancy and Nancy's mother. The court is going to decide who will keep Nancy. Ma'am and Nancy were both crying. (Ma'am either cries or cusses when she's upset.) When the Wild One saw Nancy crying, he cried as well.

Sir quieted them all. He told Ma'am that she isn't going before a Yankee military court, but before a civil court judge they know. "He is one of us," he said. "He's not going to take a child out of a good home. A child we have taken care of all of her life." Nancy stopped crying, and so did the Wild One.

I hope the magistrate makes Nancy go with her own mother, because Nancy is too fool to know how lucky she is.

Saturday, June 10, 1865

Dear Friend,

Nancy is miserable. She is afraid she'll have to go with her mother. I don't feel sorry for her.

Ruth was paid her wages today, ten dollars, and she was so happy. Mister Joe had to go to the store for Sir and was taking Ruth and Luke with him. Luke chattered about it all morning. He'd never been to a store, nor had I. In the past, most of the things we needed were made right on Davis Hall. Anyway, during slavery time, we were never allowed to leave the plantation, except to walk down the road to St. Philip's on Sunday mornings.

Ruth even put on her Sunday dress. "If anyone

looks for me, Patsy, you tell them I went to the store and I'll be back."

I nodded, but I must have looked so sad. She asked me whether I'd emptied the chamber pots and made the beds. I nodded, yes, then she said, "Oh, gal, come on with us. Anybody say anything, I'll say I need you to help me."

"Come on, little daughter," Mister Joe said as I limped up into the cart. He talked the whole time we rode into town.

We passed small farms with stick-and-mud houses and tiny cabins. Mister Joe told us they belonged mostly to poor white farmers. The whole family is working the fields. Then we rode past a larger farm, seemed almost as big as Davis Hall. The forest was pushed way back and the black laborers were working the cotton fields. Did Reverend McNeal preach at this farm, too?

The town was so very exciting. There is the store, in a white frame house, with a warehouse behind it, a mill, and a blacksmith shop. Mule and horse carts were tied to a railing that wound around the store. Some fancy horse and buggies sat on the other side of the road, shaded by large oak trees.

When we walked inside the store, it felt like Christmastime. It was crowded with people and so many things to buy! Luke's eyes got so big, I thought they'd pop out of his head. My eyes were probably popping, too. Ruth's mouth was wide open. The only one who acted like they had sense was Mister Joe. He walked up to the man who was selling things, while me, Ruth, and Luke stared all around us as if we were fool.

Oh, there were so many things, my Friend. Calico cloth in pink and blue, not like the plain homespun we always wear. I wiggled my toes as I stared at the beautiful slippers — some in yellow, others green. There were combs, ribbons, and soaps. Imagine not having to make your own soap. And there were jars overflowing with lemon drops and peppermint drops like Sir and Ma'am give us for Christmas. I saw sardines in cans, little silver brushes and mirrors, and beautiful chamber sets, with blue and white bowls and basins.

But, Friend, the thing that caught my eye was sheets of paper I could cut and add to you, so that I don't use you up, and bottles of ink and pen nibs.

Ruth asked what she could buy for me — beautiful calico for a kerchief or candy. I shook my head, but she kept on, telling me she wanted to buy me something nice because I been such a big help to her. She offered me a beautiful lace handkerchief and a pretty little hand mirror. I wanted the paper and pen so much. I thought about how I wanted to be more like Ruth and Cook and speak up for myself.

I pointed to the stack of paper.

"What you want paper for?"

I was so rattled trying to tell my secret I stammered worse than ever.

Then Mister Joe spoke for me the way everyone always does. "I think daughter means she wants some paper for to write on when the school start."

But Ruth just said I could get paper later on and bought me some lemon drops and material for a kerchief.

My heart and my head hold so many words and thoughts, but my mouth is like a jailer that won't release them. Friend, I have to find a way to make Ruth and everyone else understand that I am not a dunce, though I felt like one today.

Sunday, June 11, 1865

Dear Friend,

At first the day began as a mighty disappointment because I could not go to the arbor. I had to help Nancy take care of the children. Nellie is growing teeth and frets all of the time. The Wild One has a fever. While Nancy was in the chamber putting cold compresses on his forehead, I took the baby into the library.

If anyone asked me why, I planned to say because it was cool in there and she was fretful everywhere else. I am still ashamed of myself for not speaking up yesterday at the store. I am free now. Why do I still keep this secret?

My heart danced when I found the *Goody Two-Shoes* book on the desk. I opened it, sat myself down on the floor, and rocked the cradle as I read.

Every time Nellie whimpered, I stuck my pinkie in her mouth so she'd have something to chew on. If Nancy saw me, I wasn't going to hide what I was doing. And if Ma'am or Sir found me, I would say I was reading Nellie a story. Are you laughing, Friend? I am.

At least I was brave for a little while today, Friend.

Tomorrow, Ma'am and Nancy go before the magistrate.

Monday, June 12, 1865

Dear Friend,

Mister Joe was the coachman again today. He drove Nancy, Ma'am, and Sir to the magistrate this morning. I was hoping that Nancy would change her mind and go with her mother. How could she be so foolish and not accept her own mother?

It seemed as though many hours passed before I saw the carriage coming up the road. Nancy, dressed in one of Ma'am's old frocks, had a big smile on her face. Ma'am was smiling, too. I knew then that Mary Ella, Nancy's mother, was probably somewhere crying.

Mister Joe told Ruth the whole story. The magistrate wanted to know where Mary Ella lives and what she does for work. She is a nurse and a laundress and lives in a stick-and-mud house provided by the Yankee Army for the people who work for them. She told the magistrate that Nancy had lived with her until she was four years old, then Mistress Davis took her to live in The House even though Mary Ella begged her not to.

The magistrate said that because Mary Ella was the slave of Thomas Davis, Nancy belonged to him and his wife and they had the right to take her in those days. When the magistrate asked Nancy, "Is this woman your mother?" she just said she didn't know and that she wanted to stay with her mistress. The magistrate declared Nancy a bound servant who has been treated well by the Davis family. She will remain in their care until she is eighteen years old.

Am I a bound servant until I am eighteen? I wonder. I suppose so. But if my mother or father appears at the gate, I will beg the magistrate to let me go.

Wednesday, June 14, 1865

Dear Friend,

Ruth went to the cabins again last night. She still doesn't say why she's going, and I'm afraid that the Union League she and Mister Joe talked about are making plans to leave Davis Hall.

It rained all day today. Ma'am scolded me for taking so long to iron. She says I should be able to wash and iron all in the same day. Ruth helped me as best she could, but she has so much of her own work. She is so nice to me. This morning as we cleaned Sir's chamber, I tried again to tell her that

I could read and write. But when I stuttered she just said, "Patsy, don't upset yourself so."

Friend, I lowered my head and kept sweeping so she couldn't see the water welling up in my eyes. Why can't I make her understand what I am saying? I will have to show her.

Saturday, June 17, 1865

Dear Friend,

The teacher must be coming soon. Ruth and I went to the quarters for a few hours and helped Violet and the other women finish cleaning the spinning house. The men made a long bench and Brother Solomon donated a small table for the teacher.

Douglass and another young man finished whitewashing the walls. Friend, if I could speak without sputtering I would have told him I prayed that his friend, Richard, is safe. I just smiled when he walked into the spinning house and said hello to everyone.

I felt good anyway, listening to the women gossip as I polished the bench and the teacher's table with beeswax. Their stories were almost as good as

Mister Joe's. Violet knows everyone's business in the quarters just like Ruth knows everyone's business in The House. Some of the families are leaving for the sea islands tomorrow. They believe they will get land. "I think they foolish, myself," Violet said. "Should wait till the end of the year. Land ain't going nowhere."

I was relieved when Ruth agreed. "No sense leaving with empty pockets," she said. So Ruth will stay a while, too.

As I sit in my chamber (storeroom) writing to you, Friend, I am thinking now that perhaps I will wait until the teacher comes and show her how well I can read, then she can tell Ruth. It will be so wonderful having lessons like Annie and Charles. And best of all I won't have to sneak and hide.

I just had another thought, Friend. I hope Douglass and his mother and sister are not one of those families leaving.

Sunday, June 18, 1865

Dear Friend,

Today was wonderful! The first wonderful thing was, I scolded Nancy good. This morning she called me stupid. I told her *she* acted stupid when she treated her mother like an old head rag. I stammered it out good and clear.

Then I put on my cleaned and ironed homespun Sunday dress and wrapped my head in the new kerchief Ruth gave me and hurried to the arbor before Miss Sarah asked me to mind Nellie.

The next wonderful thing was Douglass is still here. But the most wonderful news, my Friend, is a teacher will come the beginning of July. Finally! Reverend McNeal told us this morning. He also said that the Freedmen's Bureau will supply books, slates, and desks, and that the spinning house will do until we build a real school.

We are overjoyed. July cannot come fast enough.

Monday, June 19, 1865

Dear Friend,

Mister Joe stopped by the kitchen shed this morning after shaving Sir. He said that Brother Solomon is not telling Sir when people leave. The hands who remain will take their places. Though it means additional work, it means more money for them when they get their share of the crops. I pray that the families who left the coast get there safely.

Too tired to write much else. Today was wash day. I wonder how many stains Ma'am will find tomorrow.

Dear Friend,

Sir left for Charleston today. I'm sure he went to find the teacher for us, since there are already schools for black children there. I'm sure one of those teachers will be kind enough to come here and teach us.

Ruth went to the quarters again last night, and I stayed with Luke until she returned. It's every Tuesday lately. Now that we almost have a school, I'm not so worried about her leaving. I don't think anyone else is leaving for a while.

Dear Friend,

My secret is out! This morning while Ma'am, Sarah, and Nancy were in the garden with the children, and Ruth and I cleaned the library, a feeling came over me that I could make her understand that I knew how to read. I took the *Goody Two-Shoes* book off the little partner's desk and began to read aloud:

> "'Little Goody Two-Shoes, set forth at large
> for the benefit of those,
> Who from a State of Rags and Care,
> And having Shoes but half a pair;
> Their Fortune and their Fame would fix,
> And gallop in a Coach and Six.'"

"Patsy! You really reading? Oh lord, girl, you can actually read? And you ain't stammering and stuttering?"

She hugged me so hard, I nearly lost my breath. Then she held me at arm's length. "Now you ain't playing with me, are you? You not just making believe?"

I shook my head. I told her how I'd learned. But I told her that I didn't want anyone to know because it was against the law when I taught myself to read.

She said I could show Luke and some of the other children. I could show her. I couldn't get a word in. I just kept saying, "But-but-but," and Ruth kept chattering.

"Maybe you're right, Patsy. Let Missus Davis

keep thinking you ain't got no sense, otherwise she'll give you more work and you won't have no time to teach me and Luke to read."

I'm sorry, Friend, but I have to take a page from you so that I can write the alphabet for Luke and Ruth. We had our first lesson tonight. Ruth says she will buy paper, ink, and pen nibs on Saturday when she gets all of her wages. She says I'm like a little jewel that almost got lost under a pile of rags. Sometimes Ruth says very funny things.

Saturday, June 24, 1865

Dear Friend,

I am teaching Ruth and Luke one letter at a time as I saw the teacher do with Annie and Charles. I point to the letter and tell them its name and they repeat after me. Luke noticed that the letters don't get stuck in my mouth the way words do. Ruth and I laughed. I also wrote their names for them: Ruth Johnson and Luke Johnson.

Ruth is like a mad woman. She rushed out of the kitchen this morning, and when she returned with Luke a few hours later, they had packages of paper, ink, pens, and nibs. I think Ruth spent all of her wages. Luke's cheeks bulge with lemon drops.

Dear Friend,

I have added pages to you with the paper Ruth gave me. I cut the paper in half so that the pages are exactly your size, and I've taken a piece of the string we use for candle wicks and tied the pages inside your back cover. I also found a piece of purple ribbon in the rag box to tie around the string. You look quite pretty, my Friend.

Reverend McNeal was not at the bush arbor this morning. He was preaching at one of the other farms. When it was time for people to give thanks and speak their minds, Ruth thanked God for the gift of a wonderful child. I thought that she was talking about Luke, but she pointed to me. "This girl can read and write as good as any teacher." (How did Ruth know that? I wonder.)

I wanted to hide my face, Friend, when everyone gathered around me as if I was someone special. Violet's eyes practically popped out of her head in surprise when she asked how I learned.

"Yes, tell us," Douglass said, and smiled at me. My heart danced, and I looked pleadingly at Ruth. I wasn't accustomed to people making a fuss over me. Ruth understood and explained for me.

Friend, I promise that I will try harder to speak

for myself, but I was too excited and surprised to talk. Let me tell you a secret, though. I felt like a little queen this morning with everyone making a fuss over me — especially Douglass.

Monday, June 26, 1865

Dear Friend,

I am very much like Goody Two-Shoes. Now I will teach other children how to read, and some grown-ups, too.

Ruth has gone mad for reading. She practices the letters all day. If she sees a word on a box or a tin, she will ask me to read it for her and tell her the names of the letters. Old newspapers are saved from the fire now. Ruth has a growing stack of papers in her cottage.

As you know, Friend, today is wash day and I had so much work to do. With the baby, every day is wash day for her linen. Thank goodness the Wild One knows how to take himself to the chamber pot.

Luke was too sleepy tonight to look at letters. He fetched water all day for me, along with his other chores. Even Ruth was too worn out to memorize new letters tonight or have me read a little bit of the paper to her and Luke. I have moved back into their cottage. Ruth says that I can write and burn the candle all night if I wish to.

Friend, I am so happy these days. Ruth isn't talking about leaving, and July is just next week. That means a teacher!

Tuesday, June 27, 1865

Dear Friend,

Ruth went to the cabins again tonight. I showed Luke some more letters. He learns very fast and knows from A to F. He and Ruth are also writing the letters as they say them, and they are practicing writing their names as well.

Sunday, July 2, 1865

Dear Friend,

Our worship was short this morning. Reverend McNeal spoke a few words and told us people from his church in Baltimore were collecting books to send to the plantation schools.

We sang a few songs and prayed before the men and women went back to the fields.

This is the busiest time of year, when the cotton plants have to be thinned so that they stand five feet apart. Mister Joe says that the hands have to struggle with the earth to bring in a good crop. The hands belong to the fields now and have little time for anything else.

Brother Solomon said that before Sir left for Charleston, he noticed that there seemed to be fewer people. But Brother Solomon told him that the fields were so fertile and large with plants, it just seemed that way.

Before they went back to work, Violet and several other women asked me to stay with the older children and show them their letters.

We sat in a circle in the clearing under the arbor and I drew letters in the dirt with a stick. The old women who take care of the children made sure that the littlest ones were quiet, even though they were too young to learn ABCs.

Luke and Ruth sat next to me on a log and showed off what they already know. The elderly women and men recited the letters as well. Friend, I felt like a teacher. Until a real teacher comes here, I suppose I'll do. Are you laughing, Friend? I am.

It's July. The real teacher will be here any day now.

Dear Friend,

No teacher yet, but I have finally discovered why Ruth goes to the cabins every Tuesday night. People from the North called Republicans (Ma'am and Sir hate them) have an organization that helps the freed men and women learn about government and voting and such things. So that's what a Union League is. Ruth said that there are Union League groups all over the South now and many freed people belong to them.

Reverend McNeal started a Union League at Davis Hall. Even though he can't always come on Sundays, he's been having meetings here every Tuesday. He also has meetings on the farms in the neighborhood. He talks to the hands about their rights and about what has happened since the War ended.

He also reads the newspaper to them. Well, this evening Reverend McNeal sent word that he could not come.

"Patsy, we really need you," Ruth said as she led me quickly across the lawn. The crickets filled the warm night with their songs.

I started to feel frightened. Suppose the paper Reverend McNeal read was too difficult for me?

Everyone will surely be angry with me, I thought. But I couldn't say no to Ruth. And if I didn't read the paper, she might begin to think about leaving Davis Hall again.

Brother Solomon and Violet's tiny cabin was stuffed with people. I saw only a small patch of the earthen floor. Several children and Luke were curled up in a corner fast asleep.

Mister Joe, Douglass, and a few other men had to sit outside the open door, but they could hear everything. I tried to find the determination and will not to be fearful — especially since Douglass was there.

Brother Solomon handed me the paper. "Little daughter, now you just try to do the best you can. If there's something you don't know how to read, we understand."

I felt less anxious. Then he told me that Reverend McNeal had read up to the part where people were looking for relatives. This week he was going to read about a freed men's school that was burned down.

I sat on the bench, squeezed in with Violet and four other people. The name of the paper is the *Colored American*. I found the story Brother Solomon was talking about, and Friend, I am proud to say that I was able to read every word of it. But it made all of us so sad. A freed men's school on a plantation was burned down, and the teacher, a white Northern schoolmarm, had to flee for her life.

Another teacher from the North was pelted with stones every time she entered the schoolhouse. A soldier had to stand guard outside. Is Sir having trouble finding a teacher to come out here? I wonder. I hope not.

Then I read the section of another paper, the *South Carolina Leader*, where people write advertisements, looking for relatives. They asked me to read each one, in case there was information about one of their loved ones.

There are no sections like this in the papers Sir reads. I kept one. The advertisement says:

Information Wanted of Mary Young, who was living in Summerville in 1861, and belonged to Mrs. Edward Lowndes, but was afterwards sold to Mr. Colder, and carried up the country, perhaps to Spartensburg or Columbia. Any information respecting her whereabouts thankfully received by her son, Thomas S. P. Miller, at Charleston, S.C.

When I finished reading, Violet said she thought I just knew the letters and a few words here and there. I thought Ruth was going to shake Violet.

"I told you she knows everything about reading and writing!" Ruth said proudly.

Brother Solomon told me not to say anything about these meetings to anyone at The House. I promised not to. Ruth said, "She a fine girl and knows better than to lick her mouth all over the place."

By the way, Friend, today used to be a holiday. Ma'am says it means nothing to the people of the South now.

Wednesday, July 5, 1865

Dear Friend,

Ruth and Luke have memorized the letters up to J, along with a matching word for each letter. I cannot write much tonight, since I am so tired after last night. But I am very excited. Mister Joe will be picking up Sir at the dock on Friday morning. I hope the teacher likes us.

Thursday, July 6, 1865

Dear Friend,

I'm so tired. Ma'am worked Ruth and I hard today. We had to wash the windows, polish the furniture and the floors, besides doing our regular tasks. Ma'am wanted everything just so for Sir's return.

Luke and Ruth are already fast asleep. Good night, Friend.

Friday, July 7, 1865

Dear Friend,

What disappointment today. Sir returned from Charleston without a teacher. It turns out he went there to take an oath and swear his loyalty to the United States government.

Friend, I don't know what made me think that he was getting a teacher, except I wanted one to come so much. Mister Joe says that he's sure the Freedmen's Bureau will be sending a teacher this month, as the Reverend promised. I hope he is right.

Sir is sick with some kind of fever. Ma'am says it's because of Yankees and unfaithful people like

James, Cook, Miriam, and all of the field hands who deserted them in their time of need.

I know Ma'am misses Cook more than ever now that Sir is sick. Ruth sent Luke and me to the woods behind The House to pick some snakeroot for Sir's fever. Luke spotted it first. We pulled it out of the ground and brought it back to Ruth.

She took the bottle of whiskey out of the pantry, poured a lot into an empty jar, and stuck the root inside. The roots look like long pieces of thread.

"This is how Cook used to do it, I think," Ruth said. Then she laughed, "If it don't cure him, at least it'll make him happy."

Luke knows all of his letters up to N and can write his name. Ruth is so proud of him. Friend, I am trying to get over my disappointment and just keep hoping that maybe a teacher will come sometime this month.

Sunday, July 9, 1865

Dear Friend,

Another disappointment today. I couldn't go to the bush arbor and teach the children. Nellie is fretful again so they could not take her out, and Sir wanted either Nancy or me to be around in case he needed anything. He is feeling a little better, he says. Maybe it's the snakeroot.

When Ruth returned, she said the children asked for me. They called me the ABC girl. I like that name.

Reverend McNeal preached today, but he will not be able to be here on Tuesday. Ruth asked me to read for them again. "You the only one who can help us," she said.

Monday, July 10, 1865

Dear Friend,

I was able to do all of the washing and begin some of the ironing — all in a day. Luke helped me and recited his letters. He knows up to Q now, and we spelled small words.

Tuesday, July 11, 1865

Dear Friend,

Brother Solomon announced that Reverend Mc-Neal's life has been threatened because of his political activities. He will stop coming to the plantation and to the farms for a while, except on Freedmen's

Bureau business when he can have a soldier to guard him.

"We can still have our meetings because we have our little reader to help us out," Brother Solomon smiled at me.

Friend, sometimes I just read the words and do not know what they mean. But after Douglass and Brother Solomon and the others discuss it, I understand a little. Some of the Republicans want the freed men to have the right to vote. Only the men can vote, not the women.

I don't know why women can't vote, too. The women on Davis Hall (except for Nancy, Ma'am, and Sarah) work just like the men do.

I like to read the advertisements because maybe one day I will read one that says "looking for information about a girl named Patsy who walks with a limp."

Wednesday, July 12, 1865

Dear Friend,

The teacher should be here soon. So today Luke and I swept the spinning house and wiped the bench and the teacher's table. Then Luke said, "Patsy, you be the teacher." I stood behind the little table and Luke sat on the bench. We played school for a little while. He knows his letters now from A–Z and recited them all. I'm so proud of him. We were just playing, but it almost felt real to me.

Thursday, July 13, 1865

Dear Friend,

I heard the best news. Reverend McNeal came to the plantation today to tell us that the Freedmen's Bureau has found a teacher for us! She will be here on Friday, July 28. Luke is so excited. He can't wait to show the teacher how much he already knows. Now I really must find myself a suitable second name.

Friday, July 14, 1865

Dear Friend,

Somehow Mister Joe found the time to make a chair to put behind the teacher's table. It seems kind of little and rickety, so I hope the teacher is thin and small.

Sunday, July 16, 1865

Dear Friend,

It was a pretty morning. The sky so blue, trimmed with soft puffs of white clouds. When I went to the bush arbor, the children were waiting for me. They have remembered only a few letters. But one little girl remembered all of the letters I had shown them, up to E. Some of the children pay attention, but others are too little. One of the old women swats a little boy like a fly every five minutes to keep him quiet.

Everyone is so excited because we will soon have a real school and a real teacher.

Monday, July 17, 1865

Dear Friend,

Today I was able to wash and do half the ironing, too. All by myself.

I think if Luke had a book, he would learn how to read. He is able to pick out words from the old newspapers Ruth and I collect. He can read simple words like *one*, *and*, *the*, and *two*, and he and Ruth know how to read and write their names.

Tuesday, July 18, 1865

Dear Friend,

There is no Union League meeting this evening.
Mister Joe didn't have time to buy a paper. The
men and women are exhausted. They work until it
is completely dark. Ten more days, but I am trying
not to get too excited over the teacher this time because I don't want to be disappointed again.

Sunday, July 23, 1865

Dear Friend,

I brought paper and a pen with me to the arbor
this time and wrote some of the children's names
for them on paper that I cut into small pieces, so
every child could have one. When the teacher
comes on Friday, she will be surprised to see that
some of the children have begun to learn their letters. A few can already spell their names!

Tuesday, July 25, 1865

Dear Friend,

There was no meeting tonight either. Ruth says that some people think they should not be concerned about politics and voting. They should worry only about schools and land.

The sun feels as if it has tongues of fire that lick your face and back. The only children who are playing are the very little ones. Every child is in the field carrying water to the hands. Everyone has to work in order to get a decent crop. Ruth even let Luke carry water to Mister Joe.

Wednesday, July 26, 1865

Dear Friend,

Today Nancy saw Luke sitting at the table in the shed studying new words I'd written for him. She asked him what he was doing. He told her that he was learning his letters. I continued to wash the rice, making believe that I didn't hear a thing. "Who show you how to read?"

"Patsy," he said. Nancy laughed all the way down the passageway and back to The House. I don't care about Nancy laughing. I know the truth.

I can read and write and she can't. Will she go to school with the rest of us? I wonder.

Dear Friend,

When I saw Reverend McNeal walk through the gate escorted by a Yankee soldier, I knew that the teacher wasn't coming. They walked toward the quarters, and Ruth and I followed them.

People left the fields when they saw the Reverend. "No one will board the teacher," he explained.

The family she was going to live with was threatened by their neighbors when they found out that the teacher was a Northerner who was going to teach in a school for black children. Several neighbors said that they would burn down the family's house. Other families are now afraid to take the teacher in. Many of the Southerners say that the Northern teachers are troublemakers, filling the heads of the freed people and their children with dangerous ideas.

Reverend McNeal promised that his church would try to send down a black teacher who could live with a black family.

"Unfortunately," he said, "it would be unthinkable in these times for a black teacher to board with a white family, or a white teacher to board with a black family. But this is not the end; it is still only the beginning. You will have a school. Our church will still send you the books, and a teacher as well."

Ruth and I walked slowly back across the lawn with Luke skipping in front of us. Ruth said, "My Luke is going to school. I'm not staying here to keep living like a slave."

Her words sound in my ears still as I write. Ruth and Luke are snoring softly and the crickets are singing. There will never be a teacher or a school here at Davis Hall.

But tonight, even though we are upset about the teacher, I still went over the letters with Ruth and Luke. They have learned everything I taught them.

Could I bring children from the quarters to the spinning house on Sundays perhaps, and show them their letters until a real teacher comes? I could read them stories from the books the Reverend is sending to us. It would be almost like a school.

Friend, this is probably a fool thought. I am no teacher, but I'm so afraid Ruth will leave if I don't do something soon.

Dear Friend,

This morning as Ruth and I prepared breakfast I asked her if I could show the children their letters in the spinning house.

At first she seemed as if she didn't understand me, but I wouldn't give up. "Until, until, the real teacher comes."

Suddenly, dimples decorated her face. This is what she said: "Patsy, yes, yes. Of course. Lord, here we is with a teacher all along and looking for someone on the outside." She snatched me by the shoulders so hard, I thought she was going to fling me across the yard. "Oh, Patsy, what you mean until the real teacher come? You are the real teacher! You the only one among us who can read and write. So, you the teacher!"

Well, Friend, Ruth is an excitement kind of person. Of course I couldn't get a word in. For a moment I felt nervous, for I am no real teacher. But Ruth said I was the teacher and rushed to the quarters to tell Violet.

I hope I don't seem foolish tomorrow when I bring the children into the spinning house.

Sunday, July 30, 1865

Dear Friend,

I almost feel like a real teacher!

At first, when I went to the spinning house, I felt anxious as the children all stared at me. I thought I'd stammer myself right out of the room. So I began by reciting the alphabet. The children repeated after me, and I calmed down some. Then I asked Luke to say his letters.

He popped up off the ground and, loud and proud as you please, recited from A to Z. Ruth stood by the door, her arms folded. She was grinning from ear to ear. I asked the other children to recite also. None knew past E and most only remembered A, B, and C.

Some of them still had the pieces of paper I'd given them with their names written on them. Since most of them had taken the last name of Davis, I taught the letter D, using the name Davis, and other easy words like *dog* and *day*. Friend, I cannot describe how happy I am when I am with the children.

Tuesday, August 1, 1865

Dear Friend,

Reverend McNeal was at the meeting tonight, so I didn't have to go and read the paper. I miss it a little though. I asked Ruth to save the section of the paper where people are looking for relatives. I like to read that. And who knows, someone might be looking for me.

Luke is already fast asleep. Good night, Friend.

Wednesday, August 2, 1865

Dear Friend,

The cotton fields are covered with ivory-colored petals. The bolls will soon open.

Still no teacher, but Mister Joe says that he thinks we might get one by September. He says, "In the meantime, we have our own little teacher." It was a nice thought that rested with me all day. But I still long to go to school. Is Mister Joe's daughter still in school? I wonder.

Sunday, August 6, 1865

Dear Friend,

We were not at the arbor very long this morning because people had to go back to the fields. The older children now have to work as well. Several of the elderly women who mind the children know some of their letters, too. They say they will help the little ones during the week, since they see them more than I do.

But now the fields come first. The cotton is ready to be picked. When I am showing the children their letters I forget all the things that worry me — Ruth leaving, someone claiming me, going to a real school, having books to read, finding a name for myself.

Wednesday, August 9, 1865

Dear Friend,

Sir is ill again, and I had to be in The House all day listening to Ma'am screech in my ear. She says Nancy and I are apprentices and she's training us. For what? I wonder.

I wish I could be trained to be a real teacher.

Monday, August 14, 1865
Wash day

Dear Friend,

I cannot stay with you long because I am writing the letters on a paper for each of the older children. I think it might help them remember.

Wednesday, August 16, 1865

Dear Friend,

Sir is still feeling poorly. The snakeroot did not work, I suppose. Ma'am says it's the heat, so she told Ruth to let Luke come to the drawing room and fan Sir. Ruth was helping me clean the chambers. Her eyes looked angry instead of soft like they usually do. Then she told Ma'am she wants Luke to be schooled and that if he stands here and fans Sir, could she in turn teach him to read and write? Let him look at a book? Ruth winked at me.

Well, Friend, I thought Ma'am would take sick like her husband. She went from white to pink to red and then turned back to white. Ma'am refused, saying she has a sick husband to tend to.

Ruth suggested that Sarah could show him.

Ma'am screeched like a jaybird. "She's got her

own children. Who is putting all of these fool notions in your head?"

Ruth continued sweeping, "I just had another fool notion," she said. "On the coast, they have plenty freed men's schools, a cook like me could always find work. Now, you have some leftover old books in the library that my boy could borrow, look at the pictures, learn what a book feels like in his hands."

She kept sweeping, and Friend, it was all that I could do to keep from laughing. Ma'am told me to gather up Annie and Charles's old books and magazines. The first book I put my hand on was the *Goody Two-Shoes* book, then the *Wonder Book* and five copies of the *Youth's Companion.*

I took them to Ma'am, and she looked them over quickly.

I was still clutching *Goody Two-Shoes*, and imagining myself reading it as often as I wished, when Ma'am took it away from me. She said it was Sir's favorite when he was a boy. He still treasures it.

My heart was heavy as I turned around and took the magazines and the other book to Ruth.

Later Ma'am told Ruth that Luke is a good child and needs to be apprenticed to a cooper or a tailor.

"He belongs to me now. I'll be the judge of what he needs," Ruth snapped.

Saturday, August 19, 1865

Dear Friend,

Sir is feeling weak, but his fever has broken. Ma'am called in Doctor Ashley. Luke is so happy that he doesn't have to fan anymore. It seems as if we spent the whole evening toting water to The House so that everyone could take their baths.

Luke and Ruth are asleep now. After we took our own baths, I spent the rest of the evening reading to Luke. He loves the stories in the *Wonder Book*.

Sunday, August 20, 1865

Dear Friend,

The children were so happy to see me this morning. They ran over when I reached the arbor. I felt as though my soul would rise and fly, as our song says.

We walked together to the spinning house. I will call it a schoolroom — even though it's not a real schoolroom, and I am not a real teacher. I gave each older child a paper with all of the letters and an easy word to match each letter, just the way Annie and Charles's teacher used to do.

If I had a slate I could begin to show some of them how to write. We are all very happy in the spinning house, I mean to say schoolroom. Luke loves to help the others, so he can show off what he already knows. I could stay there all day with the children. One of the old women said to me, "You such a quiet little thing, but you sho' know how to teach them letters."

I surprised myself when I said thank you without stammering.

Tuesday, August 22, 1865

Dear Friend,

There was no meeting tonight. Reverend Mc-Neal did not come, nor did he send word. Ruth and I hope that nothing has happened to him.

Thursday, August 24, 1865

Dear Friend,

Sir is ill again. Luke's fanning doesn't help him anymore. It's a good thing Ruth didn't hear Sir scream at Luke today. That would have caused a terrible row.

Mister Joe ate delicious okra gumbo with us this evening. No one has seen Reverend McNeal in over a week. I am afraid for him.

Luke begged Mister Joe for a story, and Mister Joe said he thought Luke was reading book stories now.

I still like Mister Joe's stories. I asked him to tell the story about the people who could fly. I stammered so much, Mister Joe laughed. "Daughter, get that word out!"

Ruth smiled at me. "Girl, you start sputtering anytime you ask for something. You go on and ask. All anyone can say is no. And how come you don't sputter when you read?" I couldn't answer. I don't know why myself.

Ruth put her arms around me. "This stammering and sputtering you do is something you can help. And don't be ashamed of how you speak."

"I think this little daughter here can speak just fine when she with people who love her," Mister Joe said.

Friend, I was so speechless, all I could do was smile. I never thought much about anyone loving me, except God and my mother and father, if I was with them. Ruth, Luke, and Mister Joe feel like my family. And by the way, I think Mister Joe has his eyes on Ruth, but she don't know it.

If Mister Joe and Ruth got married that would be a wonderful thing. Ruth and Luke would still be in the neighborhood — maybe she would still work here at Davis Hall. And Luke can go to school here when we get one.

Saturday, August 26, 1865

Dear Friend,

Sir seems to shrink each day, but as his body weakens, his mouth becomes stronger and coarser. He screamed at Ma'am, and when I served him his tea he threw some curses at me, too, because the tea was weak.

"I . . . I . . . didn't make it, Master." (I meant to say Sir, but when I said Master he calmed down.)

Another amusing thing happened today. I laugh when I think of it. The Wild One was bouncing around the drawing room like a jackrabbit and wouldn't stop. Nancy turned him on her lap and spanked him. He screamed and ran to his mother. I was wiping off the chair he'd jumped on when Sarah dashed into the room and snatched Nancy and spanked her.

Friend, Nancy sassed Sarah and then Ma'am came in the room and slapped Nancy. Sir cussed at everyone from the other drawing room. I left the room because I didn't want them to see me laughing.

Nancy didn't speak a word for the rest of the day. It serves her right after the way she treated her own mother.

Dear Friend,

I did not see the children today. Sir is ill, and I had to remain in The House to help since everyone else went to St. Philip's. I gave him his tea, and he fell fast asleep. So I went to the library to read the *Goody Two-Shoes* book.

I'm not scared anymore of anyone finding out I can read and write. But, Friend, I could not find the book at all. Ma'am must have put it away in the trunk with Sir's other childhood things.

Everyone is worried about Reverend McNeal because he still has not been seen, even on the other farms. Friend, I will pray hard for Reverend McNeal's safety.

Monday, August 28, 1865

Dear Friend,

Ruth and I both cried when Mister Joe gave us the sad news today. The Reverend was ambushed when he was traveling alone to one of the farms for a Union League meeting. He was attacked by the Regulators, who said he was trespassing on private property. He was beaten very badly and will not be coming back to Davis Hall or to any of the farms around here. He has returned to Baltimore for a while.

Mister Joe said they can still have meetings since I can read the paper to them.

"Yes," I said without a stammer. I am feeling like a different person now, my Friend. They really need me.

Wednesday, August 30, 1865

Dear Friend,

Maybe it's my imaginings, but everyone seemed so extra happy to see me at the meeting last night. Douglass sat in the cabin this time, on the ground directly in front of me. I couldn't look at him, for

I'd miss my place in the newspaper and surely stammer myself silly.

Everyone was interested in hearing about the voting and whether black men will be given the vote. Mostly, though, they care about land.

But Brother Solomon said that it is not enough to be free. If we have no vote, then we have no power. I wish I could vote myself into a school-house. It seems to me that women should be able to vote, too.

We never end a meeting without reading the Information Wanted section. I heard only breathing and crickets chirping as I read. Here is another one of the notices:

Information is wanted of my two boys, James and Horace, one of whom was sold in Nashville and the other was sold in Rutherford county. I, myself, was sold in Nashville and sent to Alabama, by Wm. Boyd. I and my children belonged to David Moss, who was connected with the Penitentiary in some capacity. Charity Moss

Will she ever find her children? I wonder. I hope so. We ended the meeting with a prayer for Reverend McNeal's recovery.

Sunday, September 3, 1865

Dear Friend,

It's September already. Will a teacher come as Mister Joe thinks? I will not be too hopeful. The old mothers and fathers call me Little Teacher now. I like that name, too.

Monday, September 4, 1865

Dear Friend,

I have done the wash and ironing all in a day. Finally. I am too tired to write very much. Ma'am said that I have become a splendid laundress. I don't like her compliments. I would rather learn how to be a splendid teacher.

Wednesday, September 6, 1865

Dear Friend,

Not as many people were at last night's meeting. Since Reverend McNeal was beaten, some of the people are saying that they do not want to be involved in politics. They are even afraid to come to Brother Solomon's cabin. Douglass says that if blacks vote then they can vote out the judges, sheriffs, and mayors who are the same men who ruled before the War and we can get the right people in office who will treat us fair and equal. I think he is right. Only women should vote, too, then that would be more votes for the right people.

Friday, September 8, 1865

Dear Friend,

This has been a day. Luke and I had just finished getting back from the dairy, and we were walking back to the kitchen when we saw a black man strolling along the front walkway leading to The House. At first I thought that it was the Reverend McNeal. Then I saw that the man wore a blue Yankee uniform, and his cap was turned a little to the side.

His black boots were polished to a high shine. He walked so straight. I didn't know that there were black Yankee soldiers. He was almost as handsome as Douglass.

Luke's round button eyes opened wide. If we hadn't had the heavy milk pails, I know Luke would've run up to him. The man strode up the walk and, instead of going to The House, he stopped at the cottages lining the walk and shouted through the open shutters of the first cottage, "Hello? Anyone home?"

"Hi, Mister Soldier," Luke yelled, trying to run. The man smiled. "Hey, boy, do you know where I could find a lady named Ruth?"

"That's my ma," Luke shouted. The soldier looked as though he was going to cry. "Let me help you with the milk pail," he said, and they walked toward the kitchen shed. I limped behind them and, before I reached the shed, I heard a yell and a crash. I knew that Ruth had dropped the skillet.

And I knew that this Yankee soldier was John, Luke's father, and that he had come to take Luke and Ruth away.

Saturday, September 9, 1865

Dear Friend,

Yesterday was the saddest day of my life as I watched Luke, Ruth, and John walk away from the plantation. They were going first to the magistrate so that they could be married by law, and then they were traveling to Charleston where John's regiment is quartered.

Ruth was so happy as she told me about their

plans. Luke was like a mad boy. It seemed as if he said, "My papa, my papa," all morning and afternoon.

While John waited in the kitchen shed, Ruth went to The House and told Ma'am and Sir that she was leaving. They were upset, but there was nothing they could do. When Ruth told them John was a soldier, they didn't say anything else. Ruth says they won't have trouble finding a new cook.

But I will have trouble finding a new friend like Ruth.

She didn't have much to pack, just two homespun dresses, a pair of trousers, and two shirts for Luke. John told her not to bring anything off this plantation except Luke and herself.

When I handed her Luke's books she refused them. "You keep these, Patsy. Luke will be going to school and so will I. We'll be getting plenty books."

I walked with them to the gate. All of the hands were there to say good-bye. Violet hugged her. I could tell that Mister Joe felt as bad as I did.

Suddenly Ruth said, "Patsy, leave. Come on with us." Before I could answer, Luke said, "Patsy, you coming, too? Who's going to teach me new words?" But John thinks it's best if I stay here, for now. When he's mustered out of the Army and they're settled, maybe I can go and live with them, he says.

Luke, Ruth, and I hugged, and I tried mightily not to cry. But when they walked out of the gate and Luke turned around and said, "I'll write you a letter, Patsy," tears rolled down my face.

I knew that I couldn't go with them even before John said so. They are a family, and I don't want to be a burden to them. I have to find my own family.

Friend, as I sit in this empty lonely cottage, I am thinking that I am supposed to stay here. But I don't know why.

Now there is only Nancy and me left.

Sunday, September 10, 1865

Dear Friend,

What a trying day this has been. The only good thing about it was that Sarah had to take care of her own children. This morning Ma'am called Nancy and me into the dining room after I had served breakfast and told us what our new tasks would be.

On Monday I will do the wash and ironing as usual. Nancy will cook and clean, but I will be her helper until a new cook is hired. In the meantime, Ma'am will show Nancy how to organize herself in the kitchen. Who is going to show Ma'am? I wonder.

Well, Friend, it was a mess. I know more about cooking than both Nancy and Ma'am. When I returned from collecting firewood as Ma'am ordered me to do, I saw her and Nancy standing at the fireplace staring at the three-legged pot for cooking rice, wondering what to do first. Nancy should have paid attention when Ruth was trying to teach her.

I started toward the arbor, but then turned around and went back to the kitchen shed. I felt sorry for them. And I had to eat, too. Ma'am was getting redder and redder. I knew she'd blow up directly. So I showed them how to properly clean the rice and the exact amount of water to put in the pot so that every grain of rice is separate and cooked just right.

I missed seeing the children today. It is so lonely without Ruth and Luke. Mister Joe didn't come for dinner, but he did bring me some firewood and water. He misses Ruth, too.

I ate alone after Nancy had her dinner. I have moved back into the storeroom because the cottage reminds me of Ruth and Luke too much.

Monday, September 11, 1865

Wash day

Dear Friend,

I am so tired, but I have to tell you this. Nancy made some rock-hard biscuits this morning. This was one time I was happy that I have become a splendid laundress, because I had nothing to do with those biscuits, and wasn't standing in the dining room when Sir broke his tooth biting into one and spanked Nancy. She was crying when she ran back into the kitchen with Ma'am following her. She must have felt sorry for Nancy. I stopped doing the wash to show Nancy how to make the hominy grits Sir was hollering for.

Tuesday, September 12, 1865

Dear Friend,

I couldn't go to the meeting tonight. There has been too much work. Sir is ill again. Maybe it's Nancy's biscuits.

Wednesday, September 13, 1865

Dear Friend,

I can't write too long for I am exhausted. I wish Luke and Ruth were still here. I have not even read my magazines or the *Wonder Book* because I became accustomed to reading with them. I hope Sir gets better soon. He is wearing us all out.

Mister Joe told me this afternoon that everyone missed me at the meeting last night. The children asked for me on Sunday. I miss them.

Now, Friend, I think I understand why I didn't go with Ruth. Had I left, who would be here to show the children their letters? And who would be here to read the paper at the meetings?

Sunday, September 17, 1865

Dear Friend,

Sir died this morning. I cannot stay and speak with you because everything is in such a state. Ma'am is in her chamber, and Nancy is there with her. Sarah is screaming at the Wild One something awful. Nobody seems to know what to do. How I wish Cook or Ruth was here. They would surely know. I am so frightened. Something must be done. We can't leave old Sir in his chamber like that. I will talk to you later.

Evening

I ran to the arbor to tell them that Sir died. Mister Joe was there, too. Violet stopped her work and walked back with me to The House.

Nancy flew down the passageway yelling at me and trying to play the mistress. Before I could say a word, Violet said, "Now, you hush your mouth. This child the only one up here had sense enough to come and get some help."

Well, Violet knows how to organize and give orders. She sat down on the bench in the kitchen shed and told Nancy and me what to do. Nancy had to stop every clock in the house, otherwise they would wind down and never work again. And I had to cover the mirrors and pictures, to keep the spirits quiet and protect the living.

Friend, The House feels sad. I could hear little moans coming from Ma'am's chamber.

I rushed back to the kitchen when I finished. Nancy must have felt the same way I did because she was already back in the kitchen when I got there.

Violet told me to get a sheet of white paper and pin a strip of black material or crepe paper at the very top. Several young people would go around the neighborhood and let Sir's friends know that he had died. His friends would sign their names on the paper. Some of the poor whites like the overseer, who knew Sir or had worked for him, would put their X mark on the paper. Many of them don't know their letters either.

Douglass took Sir's horse, so that he could get to the distant plantations and farms quickly. Violet said that a pass had to be written for him because if the Regulators see a black young man on a fine horse, they'll accuse him of stealing it.

Ma'am couldn't do it because she was grieving too much.

Friend, I spoke up. I could write a pass for him.

Nancy was too surprised to say anything stupid. I got my paper and pen out of the storeroom, and I sat at the table and wrote a pass for Douglass to go to the Cooper Plantation and the farms in that neighborhood.

I had imagined myself writing in the open for all to see, but I didn't want Sir or anyone else to die so that I could write freely.

Douglass smiled at me when I handed him the

pass. "Thank you, Little Teacher," he said. His voice still sounds in my ears.

Next, Violet told Nancy and me to go back in The House and start to clean. She walked behind us down the passageway.

As Nancy and I swept and dusted in the drawing room, I could hear the men chopping down a tree so that they could make a coffin for Sir. Ma'am's moans seemed to fill every corner of The House.

Perhaps so that she couldn't hear Ma'am, Nancy kept chattering and worrying me about how I learned to read and write. "Who teach you?"

I told her how I learned, then she asked, "You was sneaking?"

"Yes!" I answered proudly without stammering. She didn't play the mistress with me, but did her part without flouncing around and complaining.

We were both afraid to go near Sir's chambers. We heard Mister Joe in there. Violet was in Ma'am's chambers. What was she saying and doing in there? I wondered. By the time Nancy and I finished cleaning the drawing rooms and the library, the moaning had stopped, and Mister Joe and Brother Solomon carried Sir into the library and laid him out on the cooling board in his best suit.

He looked like he was sleeping, Friend, and

would sit up any minute and cuss Yankees and Republicans.

Violet led Ma'am, Miss Sarah, and the children into the drawing room. Even the Wild One was quiet as they watched over Sir.

Then Violet told Miss Sarah and Ma'am that they had to pass the children over Sir's body so no spirits harm them, and so they don't fear the dead.

Ma'am and Miss Sarah did as Violet told them to do. They stood on either side of the cooling board. Miss Sarah passed Nellie over Sir's body to Ma'am, then Violet took Nellie from Ma'am and handed her to me. Then Miss Sarah picked up the Wild One and did the same thing. He ran to Nancy after Ma'am put him down. Even the Wild One was quiet as Ma'am and Miss Sarah, holding Nellie, sat down to watch over Sir.

Tuesday, September 19, 1865

Dear Friend,

Sir was buried today. All of his friends and neighbors were in The House as Father Holmes laid Sir's soul to rest. Even the use-to-be overseer was there with his family. Brother Solomon,

Douglass, and all of the other hands came to pay their respects.

Sir was buried in the family cemetery right on Davis Hall. Ma'am cried something awful at the gravesite. When Father Holmes asked the hands to sing a song for their old master, Brother Solomon said, "We pray he is with the Father in heaven." He then turned around and walked back toward the cotton fields and the others followed him. Only Mister Joe and the old men and women remained. They sang, "Nearer My God to Thee," and when Father Holmes and all of the other white people left, Mister Joe cracked Sir's shaving mug and placed it on his grave. "Now he will have his favorite mug with him. Its spirit is freed."

I cried some because the world is so sad. I thought about my own mother and father who may be dead, and about Reverend McNeal getting hurt. I even thought about Ruth and Luke leaving. Sir never said a kind word to me, but he never hit me and didn't yell at me too much. Sir wasn't the most wicked man, I guess. Perhaps he is with the Father in heaven as Father Holmes says.

Wednesday, September 20, 1865

Dear Friend,

Everything feels different. Ma'am is very quiet. She spends most of her time in Sir's library with Doctor Ashley, going over Sir's papers and records. Mister Joe stopped by the kitchen shed this morning before he went to the fields. He hauled in the water I needed for the wash and killed two chickens for tonight's supper. Nancy helped as well, hanging the wash on the fence. I helped her clean the chickens and showed her how to put them on the spit for roasting over the fire.

The House seems quiet and empty without Sir. Nancy says she heard Sir walking in and out of the library. I told her that was her imaginings. I'm glad I sleep in the storeroom though. Sir never came near here when he was living. I doubt his ghost be tromping through here now.

Thursday, September 21, 1865

Dear Friend,

Nancy and I are cleaning and cooking as best we can. Even Sarah helped and swept the drawing rooms and cleaned the chamber where she and her children sleep.

Nancy is curious about my reading and writing. When I offered to show her how, she said Ma'am told her that reading and writing isn't important for black people.

Nancy believes her. If reading and writing isn't important, then why wasn't we allowed to learn how to do it?

I still think about Ruth and Luke. I wonder if they are in school. Friend, I am thinking again about a last name. If Luke or Ruth write to me, I don't want the envelope to say Patsy Davis. I need a name of my own.

Sunday, September 24, 1865

Dear Friend,

Brother Solomon prayed for Sir's soul at the arbor this morning, and then we sang "Free at Last." For the first time since Luke and Ruth left and Sir died, I didn't feel like a heavy stone was lying on my chest.

Maybe I feel better because Mister Joe told me he heard that Reverend McNeal is recovering from his injuries. And I know I feel better because I spent a lot of time with the younger children today. They like me to read to them from the *Wonder Book*.

The older children couldn't be there because they are working hard, picking potatoes and peas. I hope they haven't forgotten the little I've shown them.

Monday, September 25, 1865

Dear Friend,

We have a new cook — Mister Joe! Nancy and I are his helpers. Ma'am says he'll do until she finds a regular cook. Mister Joe does many things. He still goes out in the fields as well, so that he will get a share of the crops at the end of the year. I don't think we could survive without him.

Tuesday, September 26, 1865

Dear Friend,

There was a meeting tonight and I read the paper, even though I was so tired. One of the articles said that the land that was given to the freed men and women on the coast and the sea islands would be returned to the former slaveholders. Also, there will be no land for sale at reduced rates.

Brother Solomon said that the papers don't always tell what is true. I feel sorry for those families that left Davis Hall for the coast. I wonder what will happen to them now. I also wonder what happened to Miriam and her family. Everyone is worried that maybe now they won't get the land that Sir promised them. At least they are all together.

Brother Solomon and some of the others said that they had no choice but to continue to work until the crops are in, otherwise they will have labored for nothing.

And after the crops are in? Will they all leave? I won't think about it, Friend. Now I can't imagine how things would be here at Davis Hall without the people in the quarters. Without the children.

Friday, September 29, 1865

Dear Friend,

Nancy and I are being worked to death. Thank goodness Mister Joe is here to help. Ma'am still spends most of her time with Doctor Ashley, and Miss Sarah is still sweeping and minding her own children. Nancy said that Sir must be turning over in his grave if he knows that Sarah is trying to be helpful.

Ever since that spanking she got, Nancy has no use for Sarah. Friend, Nancy shocked me today and asked me whether I thought the woman who'd come here looking for her was really her mother. I told her that I was sure. Then she asked me why I thought so. Now, Friend, you know I'm not one for much talk, and it would have been too much trouble for me to stammer out the fact that Nancy and Mary Ella look just alike.

The Wild One dashed into the drawing room to hug Nancy and beg her to take him outdoors. He saved me from trying to explain my thoughts.

Sunday, October 1, 1865

Dear Friend,

Things do not feel at all the same, but everyone is going about their work. Mister Joe carried the family and Nancy to church, and I went to the bush arbor.

Brother Solomon is going to remind Ma'am that her husband promised them land as well as a share in the crop.

One old man said, "Let he get cold in he grave before you worry his widow."

Everyone is angry about not yet getting a school, but they thanked me for teaching the children some of their letters.

Violet said that she wished I could be in the spinning house every day with the children. When I told her I am not a teacher, she stood in front of me with her hands on her hips.

"Who say you ain't no teacher?" she said. "They ain't one of us here know more about reading and writing than you. So you is the teacher."

"Amen," Brother Solomon said.

What would Ma'am say if I told her that I had to teach the children and didn't have time for serving tea and cleaning the chambers? Are you laughing, Friend? I am.

Yet Violet's words sound in my ears.

Wednesday, October 4, 1865

Dear Friend,

I miss speaking to you, but lately by the time night falls, I am too tired to do anything but sleep. The newspaper articles were correct about the government returning land to the former slave owners.

Miss Sarah is overjoyed. She and her husband will get their plantation on Edisto Island back. Sir's land on the island will be returned to Ma'am as well.

Sunday, October 8, 1865

Dear Friend,

The mornings are cool, and the leaves are beginning to fall. I spent time at the arbor and the spinning house this morning.

I am happy when I am with the children, even though I still miss Luke and Ruth. Friend, why is it that when I grow to care for anyone they leave?

Douglass, the children, and everyone in the quarters will probably leave by the new year. For it doesn't seem as if there'll ever be a school here. September has come and gone. I don't think the people will get the land Sir promised them.

Thursday, October 12, 1865

Dear Friend,

Sarah and the children left today. Mister Joe will carry them to the docks so that they can take the boat to Charleston. The Wild One cried after Nancy, and Nellie smiled and stretched out her hands for me to pick her up. Maybe those children are like Nancy. They get used to whoever takes care of them. Black and white don't much matter to them.

Ma'am says I can sleep in The House now if I wish — in the ironing room. But I'd rather stay here. At least I can write to you and read in peace.

Saturday, October 14, 1865

Dear Friend,

The fields are still white with cotton. Ma'am is handling everything as Sir did. Brother Solomon, though, is the one who is really taking care of things. He is teaching her about the crops, the weather, and how the cotton is ginned and baled.

Sunday, October 15, 1865

Dear Friend,

It rained today, and Ma'am stayed home from church. She kept me so busy serving her tea, I didn't get to the arbor. But when Mister Joe came to start the supper, he told me that I didn't have to help him and to go to the spinning house because the children were looking for me. They didn't go to the fields because of the rain.

Monday, October 16, 1865
Wash day

Dear Friend,

Doing the laundry is much easier now. There's only me, Nancy, and Ma'am, but I am also cleaning and cooking more. Mister Joe divides his time between the kitchen and the fields. Nancy is like a noontime shadow, following behind Ma'am. Does she still think about her own mother? I wonder.

Tuesday, October 17, 1865

Dear Friend,

There was a meeting tonight, and I had to read the paper once again. I read them many articles, but the one that excited everyone was the article describing a black convention that will be held in Charleston, in Zion Church in November. It is for the black people of South Carolina to find ways to develop and protect themselves.

The part of the article I liked best and that I kept said: "We urge the parents and guardians of the young and rising generation, by the sad recollection of our forced ignorance and degradation in the past, and by the bright and inspiring hopes of the future, to see that schools are at once established in every neighborhood; and when so established, to see to it that every child of proper age is kept in regular attendance upon the same."

If Ma'am is supposed to be my guardian and Nancy's guardian then shouldn't she be giving us schooling?

Brother Solomon said that it would be so wonderful if at least one person from the plantation could go to the convention, so that people from Davis Hall would be represented, too. But that's impossible. No one can be spared from the fields, and no one has money to travel to Charleston.

But Mister Joe saved the day. He has a sister in Charleston and he will go if someone works his acres for him. Douglass, his sister, and another young man have agreed to help Mister Joe.

Oh, Friend, I wish I could be there, too. Riding in a coach and six, like Goody Two-Shoes, and stepping out, walking straight as you please to speak out for myself and say without stammering, "We must have a school at Davis Hall." Sometimes my imaginings are silly, my Friend.

Monday, October 23, 1865

Dear Friend,

Nancy shocked me today. She asked Mister Joe whether the Yankee regiment was still quartered near here. It is. I think Nancy is wondering if her mother still works for the regiment.

The year is drawing to an end. I feel anxious for the future, my Friend. Today as I watched the leaves fall, little by little, Cook's words sounded in my ears. "If I stay here I'll never know I'm free."

Tuesday, October 24, 1865

Dear Friend,

No meeting tonight because Mister Joe did not have time to buy a paper.

I was hanging the skillet over the fireplace when a wonderful thing happened. Douglass walked up to the kitchen shed and asked me to write down the letters from A to Z for him. I told him what each letter was and tried mightily not to stammer, but of course I did, even though I never stammer when I am showing people their letters. He thanked me and said that he'd come back for another lesson, until he remembered them all. I am so happy Nancy was not around.

Wednesday, October 25, 1865

Dear Friend,

I am so tired of all this work. This morning as I emptied the chamber pots, I felt as though I wanted to break each one and march up to Ma'am and tell her that I have no time for chamber pots and laundry. I have children to teach.

I completed my chores very quickly and found

Mister Joe. He said if anybody looked for me he'd say he sent me to the dairy, or to do a chore for him.

I stayed with the children until noon. Friend, half of them know most of their letters.

When Violet and Brother Solomon left the fields for their noon meal, they saw me and the children in the spinning house. With a big smile on her face, Violet stepped inside and put her hands on her hips like she always does when she has something important to say.

"Daughter, I has a mind to go right up to that house and tell that woman that you is our teacher and we has a school down here, and you don't have no time to be up in there emptying chamber pots and sweeping floors."

Brother Solomon kind of rolled his eyes at her. "Now, Vi, don't go starting no confusion. You just make trouble for our Little Teacher. This too shall pass."

What did he mean by that? I wonder.

Thursday, October 26, 1865

Dear Friend,

Ruth would be proud of me. Again, today after doing my chores I spent the rest of the morning in the spinning house teaching the children. Even Douglass came in at noon when the hands had their lunch rest. "I need you to refresh my remembrance on some of these letters, Little Teacher."

You know my heart danced and jumped. All we need now are books. I hope the people from Reverend McNeal's church send them as they promised.

Wednesday, November 1, 1865

Dear Friend,

Today is drizzling and chilly. Mister Joe has promised to bring me back a gift when he returns from Charleston. Imagine a gift and it's not even Christmastime. He will also buy slates for the children so that they can learn to write.

I want to ask him if he is going to see his daughter, but I am not supposed to know his business. I will miss him. I hope he returns. I don't want to lose yet another friend.

Monday, November 6, 1865

Dear Friend,

Ma'am is fit to be tied. Mister Joe told her that he's going to Charleston, but when he said he had to go to see about his brother, who is ill, she calmed down some.

"Daughter," he said, "sometimes you have to tell a little black lie. I don't have a brother in Charleston. I have a sister. But I don't want to put no bad mouth on her."

I was sitting at the table and cutting up an onion while Mister Joe washed the rice, and he told me about his daughter, the same story Ruth told. But I listened as though I was hearing it for the first time. "She beautiful and she smart just like you," he said proudly.

He promises that he is coming back.

Wednesday, November 8, 1865

Dear Friend,

Mister Joe left today. That heavy stone is lying on my chest again. When I saw his mule cart clanging down the road, I wanted to leave, too. I want to feel free, as though I can truly do as I please. The only time I feel free is when I am in the spinning house with the children. There is only one more month left in this year. What will the new year bring? I wonder.

Thursday, November 9, 1865

Dear Friend,

There are so many things to do now that Mister Joe is gone. Nancy and I have to cook, but I am the one who actually does all of the cooking. Today I made okra gumbo . . . it didn't taste as good as Cook's, of course — didn't even taste as good as Mister Joe's, but Ma'am didn't complain, and it sure tasted better than Nancy's biscuits.

I can't get away to the spinning house every day, but I did sneak away for a short time this morning. Miss Nosy Nancy asked me where I'd been. She was looking for me to help her and Ma'am beat the dust out of the drapes.

I told her I was teaching the children.

"I won't tell Mistress on you this time, Patsy."

I wish Nancy would stop saying Mistress.

Friend, I wish she would tell Ma'am that I can read and write. Nothing Ma'am can do about it now. She can't take out of my head what's already in there.

Dear Friend,

The hands are fertilizing the cotton fields with pine straw so that they will be ready for the new planting season next year. Many of the leaves are red and yellow, and the pine trees are a deep green. Even though there was a gray misty rain this morning, the trees looked like a painting.

I feel that next year nothing will be the same. I feel deep in my heart that Brother Solomon, Douglass, and all of the rest of the hands and their families will leave.

I can't imagine staying here without the children, and Douglass, and all of the people in the quarters.

There was no church in the arbor because of the weather. It is cold and rainy. People prayed and sang in their own cabins. I worshiped with Brother Solomon, Violet, and their children, and then I went to the spinning house.

I pray for Mister Joe's safe return every night.

Tuesday, November 21, 1865

Dear Friend,

No meeting again tonight. For Mister Joe is not here to get a paper, and everyone is so very tired.

Wednesday, November 22, 1865

Dear Friend,

A wonderful surprise today! As I was rushing to finish cleaning the breakfast dishes, Nancy flounced herself into the kitchen to tell me the postman left a big box by the gate and she couldn't tote it alone.

I wiped my wet hands on my apron and limped faster than Nancy walked to the gate.

Friend, it was just as I'd thought. The box was from Reverend McNeal's church and it was addressed to:

> Davis Hall Plantation School
> Davis Hall Plantation
> Mars Bluff, South Carolina

We carried the box into the spinning house. When some of the children saw me and Nancy they followed us. I opened the box, and it was like finding gold. First thing I looked for was the *Goody Two-Shoes* book, but that wasn't there. There were nursery rhymes and fairy tales though. I found a book about American history, too: *The First American History for Children.*

"I guess these ain't for Mistress. What she want with a box of old books?"

I think Nancy is hopelessly stupid. But I was too excited to be angry with her. More children strolled in and each wanted a book of his or her own. One little girl asked, "We doing ABCs now?"

I noticed Nancy looking around the spinning house. "This the schoolhouse? Who fix it so decent?"

I told her we all did. Friend, I decided to have a lesson. Some of the books were too difficult, but I found one book that suited us all, for everyone knows their letters and this book starts with ABCs. It is called *The Primer.* Nancy sat herself down, nice as you please, on the bench, along with several children and listened to me read: "This is a fat hen. The hen has a nest in the box. She has eggs in the nest. A cat sees the nest and can get the eggs."

Friend, we almost have a real school!

Thursday, November 23, 1865

Dear Friend,

I almost swooned today when Nancy asked me to teach her how to read. We made a trade. She does my chores while I work with the children in the morning. Nancy doesn't want Ma'am to know that I'm teaching her. Poor Nancy has no mind of her own.

Sunday, November 26, 1865

Dear Friend,

Mister Joe might be on his way back from Charleston. I hope so. I miss his okra gumbo and his stories. Nancy's biscuits are a little better. Violet said to me last Sunday, "I heard that gal who works with you made some biscuits that killed the old man."

Friend, I know it wasn't nice for me to laugh, but maybe if Nancy didn't flounce behind Ma'am so much, people wouldn't say such evil things about her.

Went to the arbor this morning. I also taught the children some new words. Some of them are like

Luke. They remember everything I show them. I wonder how Luke and Ruth are keeping.

Tuesday, November 28, 1865

Dear Friend,

No meeting tonight. I moved back into the cottage because it is so very cold in the evening, and Ma'am began to worry me about staying in The House. I started to tell her that there is a haunt on The House because Sir is strolling in and out of the library, and I am afraid to stay there. But it would be evil to say something like that just to frighten her. I know she's lonely in that house since Sarah and the children left and Sir is gone.

She still has her pet Nancy. Now Nancy sleeps in James's room. She won't tell Ma'am that I'm teaching her how to read and write. She doesn't want to anger her. So I give her secret reading lessons in the storeroom. Nancy doesn't play the mistress with me anymore. She doesn't remember the letters as easily as Ruth and Luke did. She loves to practice writing her name, though: Nancy Davis.

Saturday, December 2, 1865

Dear Friend,

Mister Joe has not yet returned. The bales of cotton are stacked and ready to be counted. I feel that our old life at Davis Hall is ending. I have dreams of going to a grand city like Charleston, attending a freed men's school, learning more things in books, and becoming a real teacher.

Sometimes, I regret not leaving with Ruth. Maybe I should have begged John to please let me go with them.

Tuesday, December 5, 1865

Dear Friend,

There was a Union League meeting tonight. Douglass brought the paper. When I sat on the bench he handed it to me and pointed to the name. "I don't know every letter, Miss Patsy, but it looked like one of the papers we been reading."

I smiled to steady my stammering and my reeling heart as I told him it was the right one. "The *South Carolina Leader*," I said, pointing to each word.

Sunday, December 10, 1865

Dear Friend,

No more field work on Sundays. The cotton is almost ready to be tallied and the people given their share. Every day I look for Mister Joe to ride through the gates. I hope he is well and nothing has happened to him. Thinking again about a suitable name for myself.

Monday, December 11, 1865

Dear Friend,

Mister Joe returned today, and he brought me a book! *The Third Freedmen's Reader.* He also brought me paper and pen nibs.

He is so full of stories about Charleston and the convention. He saw so many educated black men there, a few from the North. He also explained that there have always been free black people, like him and his family, who live in Charleston, even during slavery times. Many of them are educated, and a number of them work as blacksmiths, barbers, tailors, and at other trades. He explained that now that all blacks are free, the state put restrictions on those trades. His real trade is a barber. But now he must pay money and have the special license to be a barber. There's new laws about what blacks can do and not do. These laws are called the black codes.

But he told me not to worry because that's why they had the convention. The blacks are free now, and they going to fight against all the codes and laws.

He explained how beautiful Charleston is even though it was torn up some during the War. And he saw his daughter. She is almost finished with her schooling.

Friend, I must go now so that I can read my new book.

Tuesday, December 12, 1865

Dear Friend,

I didn't read the paper at the meeting tonight. Mister Joe was the paper, telling everything about the conference from beginning to end.

I love my new book.

Friday, December 15, 1865

Dear Friend,

I have finally found a name for myself — Phillis. I am naming myself after the poet Phillis Wheatley, who I read about in *The Third Freedmen's Reader.* It begins like this:

"Phillis Wheatley, whose likeness is on this page, was brought to this country from Africa in the year 1761. She was then between seven and eight years old. She was bought by Mrs. John Wheatley, a Boston lady." Phillis didn't remember anything about her past life, like me. And she loved to read and write and became a famous poet. I think I am a lot like Phillis.

My second name shall be Frederick, like the other person I read about in my *Freedmen's Reader,* Frederick Douglass. He was a slave, too, and taught himself how to read and write in secret! He became a famous abolitionist who spoke against slavery.

Friend, this book is a treasure. And so is Mister Joe.

Saturday, December 16, 1865

Dear Friend,

Nobody knows my new name but me. I have to become used to it myself before I tell anyone. What will Ma'am say when I tell her I have two names?

Sunday, December 17, 1865

Dear Friend,

I read to the children from my new book. They enjoy the stories and the pictures. Mister Joe bought slates and chalk like he promised, so now I can teach the children to write.

Monday, December 18, 1865

Dear Friend,

How things have changed in little ways here at Davis Hall. Now, Nancy brings me the mail in case there is something for someone besides Ma'am.

The wonderful news is I received a letter today from Luke and Ruth. Nancy was as excited as me. She tried to say the sounds of the first three letters: P, A, T. She looked over my shoulder as I read, trying to see how many words she knew.

Here is the letter:

> Dare Patsy,
>
> I am fine. My mother is fine. My father is fine. We live in the city. I am in school. My teacher say I am the best one in school. I miss you. My mother say hello. Right soon. Love Luke Johnson.

It feels as if Luke and Ruth are here with me every time I read his letter. How I wish I was there in Charleston to help him. I will write him back and tell him my new name.

Monday, December 25, 1865
Christmas Day

This year, because of Sir's death, there is no celebration. I went to the quarters after Nancy and I ate supper. Every cabin has a candle burning, and people are visiting back and forth. I visited Brother Solomon and Violet. When one of his children asked whether they were going to The House for candy and fruit, he said, "This year we have the gift of ourselves. We have a lot to be thankful for this first Christmas of freedom. We have a future now."

What is my future? I wonder.

Tuesday, December 26, 1865

Dear Friend,

A wonderful thing happened today. Nancy asked Mister Joe to carry her, if he had time, to the Yankee regiment to visit her mother. She asked me not to tell Ma'am. I promised and made sure I did all of the cleaning, so Ma'am wouldn't notice that Nancy's chores weren't done.

Her mother cried when she saw her. Nancy said she was sorry for the way she had acted, and would go and see her again sometime. Nancy is a fortunate girl. Maybe she is learning some sense.

Monday, January 1, 1866
Emancipation Day

Dear Friend,

No wash today. I spent almost the whole day in the quarters. We celebrated Emancipation Day. Some people came from other farms. Violet and the other women made greens and peas and rice, for good luck, for the new year. The people who visited brought sweet potato pies and pecan pies, and we had a good time. It seems as if everyone except me and the other children made a speech about how President Lincoln had signed the Emancipation Proclamation three years ago, and what this day means to all of us.

Brother Solomon said that we had survived the miserable time of slavery and that we must have the will and determination that Reverend McNeal spoke of, to face the future. "The future cannot be as harsh as the past has been."

Brother Solomon and Douglass announced that some of the families on Davis Hall have decided to put their money from their share of the crops (when they get it) together and form an association to purchase land.

This was a wonderful day, Friend. For some reason, even though I do not know what will happen to me, I am starting to feel less anxious about the future.

Tuesday, January 2, 1866

Dear Friend,

This is the day for signing a new contract. I limped myself on out to the lawn when I saw the agent from the Freedmen's Bureau, Ma'am, and all of the people standing there talking.

Ma'am told them that they would not be getting any land. She was not going to give away or sell any of it.

I looked at Douglass and Violet and Brother Solomon and the rest. But their faces didn't show what they were thinking.

The agent had papers so the people could sign a sharecropping contract for this new year. Brother Solomon said, "No, we leaving."

Ma'am got excited. "You must sign."

Then Douglass spoke. "You didn't keep your side of the contract. We was promised land and a school. We ain't seen either one. If it wasn't for that sweet little Patsy, none of our children would've learned their letters."

Friend, my soul did rise and fly. His words still sound in my ears.

I thought Ma'am would faint. She accused Douglass of being drunk. The agent hushed her. Ma'am looked at me in a confused way.

And then Violet went right into Ma'am's face. "We didn't get that much money after all the work. Then you make us pay for them old slave cabins we living in and for the dry peck of corn and fat meat you ration out to us once a week."

Brother Solomon had to calm her down. Then he said, "I guess we will just take our chances, but we ain't signing no more contract. We leaving to-morrow."

Well, I didn't go back to The House but came here to the cottage to write to you, Friend. I feel like one of those magical Africans who can fly. I know I am young, but I can read, write, cook, wash, and teach. I should be able to find work and care for myself.

I am free, and I need to remember what Ruth said — I must learn how to ask for what I want. I am gathering my books and my Sunday homespun dress, and I am going to the cabins to ask Brother Solomon and Violet if I can leave with them. Ma'am will not miss me until the chamber pots are not emptied.

I also want to find Douglass and tell him that my new name is Phillis Frederick.

Epilogue

Phillis Frederick (Patsy) left Davis Hall with Brother Solomon and the other families. Most of the elderly freed men and women remained, saying that it was too late for them to begin a new life. They gave their blessings to those who left. Their hearts were joyful just knowing that the time of slavery had ended, and that their children and grandchildren would live as free people. Nancy, though, remained with the Davis family for the rest of her life, working for Sarah when Ma'am died in 1877.

Some of the families went on to Charleston to find work there. Brother Solomon and his wife, Violet, accepted Phillis into their family.

The Solomon family, Douglass, his mother, sister, and nine other families worked for wages on another farm near Davis Hall. They formed a land association among themselves, each family putting a portion of their earnings into a savings account in a Freedmen's Bank, so that they could accumulate enough money to purchase land.

Mister Joe continued to work on the various farms in the neighborhood, including the farm where Solomon and the other Davis Hall families lived and worked. When his daughter finished school in 1866, she left Charleston and went to live with her father.

She started a school, sponsored by The African Civilization Society, that Phillis and the other children in the farm community attended. She immediately recognized Phillis's academic abilities. With help from the Society and small donations of money for books and clothing from the families in the community, Phillis was sent to Charleston in 1867 to attend a black private school there.

Douglass's leadership abilities were also recognized. The Reverend McNeal returned to his preaching and missionary work among the emancipated men and women. He visited the farm where the families worked and remembered Douglass from Davis Hall. Reverend McNeal's denomination, the African Methodist Episcopal Church, was seeking bright young men to train for the ministry.

Douglass left for Baltimore in 1868 to be educated and trained as a minister.

Also in 1868, Brother Solomon and the other families were finally allowed to purchase land through the South Carolina Land Commission.

With the money they had saved, each family put a ten-dollar down payment on farmland divided into fifty-acre plots in Abbeville County, South Carolina.

By 1870, their village, named Libertyville, was struggling but holding on to its independence. The settlers built cabins and modest cottages and cleared an acre of land donated by Brother Solomon for a small chapel to worship in. The Libertyville Church also served as a schoolhouse.

The village had a molasses mill, a corn and wheat gristmill, and a general store, all owned and run by various village members.

In 1871, twenty-five more black families were able to either put a down payment on land, or rent land from the original eleven families. And in this year at the age of eighteen or nineteen, Phillis graduated. She could have remained in Charleston and taught at a Freedmen's School there, or on one of the coastal islands, but she went to Libertyville to be with her family.

Phillis taught in the small chapel until the men built a one-room schoolhouse in 1872. She traveled to Charleston for many summers to further her own education, but always returned to Libertyville.

Douglass returned to the village as well, ministering to the villagers and farming. Douglass and

Phillis were married in 1878. Though they had no children of their own, Phillis said that she and Douglass had all of the children of the growing village.

The church and the school both expanded, and in 1883 Phillis became the head teacher, training two other teachers. Phillis never left Libertyville or her beloved school. She also never lost her limp, but learned how to control her stammer — except when, as her students would say, "Miz Phillis be angry with us for not studyin'. She stammerin' up a storm."

Phillis lived a long and fruitful life. Up until her death in 1930, she was loved and venerated by all of the people of Libertyville.

Life in America

in 1865

Historical Note

In December 1865, eight months after the Civil War ended, Congress ratified the Thirteenth Amendment, abolishing slavery in the United States. However, this did not mean that the approximately four million formerly enslaved men, women, and children were accepted as American citizens with equal rights under the law. They were no longer enslaved, but slavery's chains were hard to break.

To aid all the people of the South, black and white, to make the transition from slavery to freedom, in March of 1865, Congress established the Bureau of Refugees, Freedmen, and Abandoned Lands, known as the Freedmen's Bureau.

A division of the War Department, the Freedmen's Bureau clothed, fed, and sheltered white and black refugees and supervised work contracts, making sure that former slaveholders paid their freed laborers. The Bureau also resettled people temporarily on abandoned farms and plantations.

Working in partnership with Northern churches,

black and white Northern benevolent organizations, and missionary societies, the Bureau helped organize freed men's schools, as well. These organizations sent thousands of Northern schoolteachers (Yankee schoolmarms) to the South where they opened day and night schools.

According to the Freedmen's Bureau records, as of July 1, 1870, there were 2,677 day and night schools, 3,300 teachers, and 149,581 students (children and adults). When there were no teachers available, freed men and women who could read and write taught others.

Many Southerners resented the teachers and other Northerners who settled in the region during Reconstruction. They viewed the influx of teachers, speculators, and businessmen as a second Northern invasion. Referring to the newcomers as carpetbaggers, people who packed up the little they had in suitcases made of carpet and headed south to make a quick profit, white Southerners accused them of taking advantage of the defeated people of the South. Those Southerners who had remained loyal to the Union were viewed as traitors to the Southern cause and were called scalawags.

Resentment, hatred, and violence, therefore, did not end with the war.

The early years of the Reconstruction Era (1865–1867) are often called Presidential Reconstruction. Even before the Civil War ended, Abraham Lincoln had devised plans for a smooth reunification of the United States. If ten percent of the 1860 voters in a former Confederate state took an oath renouncing slavery and pledging loyalty to the Federal government, the voters (white males only) would be allowed to establish a new state constitution and government. However, the leaders and officials of the former Confederacy were not allowed to vote or participate in this process. They would have to seek special presidential pardons.

By May of 1865, the new president, Andrew Johnson, pardoned many of the former Confederate leaders and returned land that they had lost during the war. As a result, a number of the same men who held power before the war began to assume leadership positions.

Laws and regulations called the Black Codes were passed that virtually attempted to reenslave the freed people. In some states, a freed man could only be employed as a farmer or a servant. A special license was needed to perform any other type of work. Artisans such as carpenters, blacksmiths, and cobblers could not work at their trades unless they purchased a license and paid an annual tax. Often they could not afford either one. People would be arrested if they refused to sign work contracts or broke a contract. Essentially, the Black Codes sought to limit all economic options of African Americans.

Bands of white men, some of them former Confederate soldiers, organized vigilante groups on the pretense of keeping the countryside safe from "dangerous blacks." These vigilantes were the forerunners of the Ku Klux Klan and other hate groups.

During this period many freed men and women left plantations in order to find relatives or to seek work other than plantation labor, in spite of the risk of being attacked or turned over to a sheriff and arrested for vagrancy. Many were killed.

It was obvious that African Americans would only be accepted as landless agricultural workers, living as though they were still in bondage.

The freed men and women, however, resisted the many ways in which Southern leaders tried to limit them. They refused to sign work contracts that did not meet their wage demands. They were also determined that their children be educated, and they refused to work on plantations that did not allow them to have a school. And even though they could not vote, could not testify in court, and could not sit on a jury, they joined the Republican party and participated in political meetings, called Union Leagues.

African Americans established their own churches and in many states, Southern and Northern, organized black conventions in order to fight for and demand protection under the law, as well as an end to the Black Codes. Most of all, the freed men and women tried to obtain land so that they could farm for themselves and be independent of white control.

Some people managed to purchase land individually; others formed land associations and pooled their money in order to establish their own communities.

In 1866, Congress passed the Civil Rights Act, which stated that all persons born in the United States were national citizens and had the right to equal protection under the law. In other words, blacks were not just freed people but citizens. President Johnson had tried to veto the bill, but Congress overrode it, and the Civil Rights Act of 1866 became the first major legislation in U.S. history to become law without a presidential signature.

The later years of Reconstruction (1867–1877) are referred to as Radical Reconstruction. Because of continuing violence and turmoil, fueled by the refusal of Southern governments to acknowledge the citizenship of African Americans, Congress passed the Reconstruction Act of 1867, which divided the Southern states into military districts and declared martial law. It also passed the Fourteenth Amendment, ratified in 1868, guaranteeing citizenship to "all persons born or naturalized in the United States." In 1870, the Fifteenth Amendment gave the vote to all male citizens "regardless of race, color or previous condition of servitude." Finally, black men could vote. Women were not given the right to vote until 1920.

Taking their new rights seriously, African Americans went to the polls, and from 1869 to 1877, elected sixteen Americans of African descent to the Congress.

Black congressmen, along with other black Reconstruction leaders elected to state legislatures, were instrumental in passing laws that helped all of the people of the South. Because of their efforts, a public school system was instituted in the South that benefited black and white children. Most Southern states had no public education before Reconstruction. Education was for the rich and the elite. (Few poor white children and their parents could read and write either.) It was during this period as well that many of the historically black colleges were founded.

By 1877, Northerners and Republicans were weary of Reconstruction and the aftermath of war. President Rutherford B. Hayes withdrew the military troops from the South, and Reconstruction came to an end.

Southern Democrats gained political power, and the progress made by African Americans during Reconstruction was effectively curtailed. Jim Crow laws enforcing segregation of blacks and whites and severely limiting the civil rights of African Americans echoed the Black Codes.

The right to vote was essentially taken away by local officials through excessive poll taxes, unfair literacy tests, and threats of violence and loss of employment. African Americans in the North and the South could only obtain certain types of work, mostly menial labor, even if they were educated.

Black Southerners, however, never ceased struggling to attain those civil and political rights due them as American citizens.

The struggles begun during Reconstruction did not end until the 1950s and 1960s with the advent of the modern civil rights movement and leaders such as Dr. Martin Luther King, Jr., Fannie Lou Hamer, and many others. This great social movement, sown from the seeds of the Reconstruction Era nearly a century prior, finally ended the last vestiges of legal segregation in the South.

.

Living conditions for many freed people improved very little during Reconstruction. Often, they still lived in shacks and wore the same ragged clothes as when they were slaves.

On the plantations, the freed women continued to perform the same tasks they did during slavery. But now they were finally paid wages, though very low, for their hard work.

"Sharecropping" was an important development of Reconstruction. The freed people who worked as farmers were given a plot of land and a share in the money made from the sale of harvested crops.

Some freed people left the plantations to try to start life afresh. A few traveled to Northern cities hoping for more job opportunities and less racial prejudice. Others set out to find relatives, and some went west to develop frontier land.

Before Emancipation, if slaves wanted to marry, they performed a traditional ritual called "jumping the broom." But these marriages were not considered legal. During Reconstruction, public weddings finally recognized the freed people's marriages by law.

A government agency called the Freedmen's Bureau sent out representatives to explain the new laws that regulated the treatment of former slaves.

The Freedmen's Bureau, working in partnership with churches, missionary societies, and other independent organizations, set up schools for the freed people. One of the most noted educators of Reconstruction was Charlotte Forten, a black woman from Massachusetts.

The History of Little
Goody Two-Shoes
was a popular book in its day.
Prior to Emancipation,
the freed people had been
punished if they
attempted to learn how
to read and write.
Now they were finally granted
the right to an education.

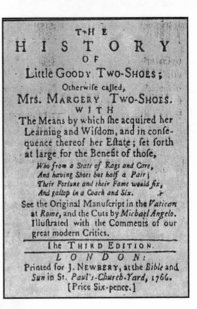

COPY OF A KU-KLUX LETTER.

Scipio.

Miss W———

We send you a picture of the way we treated
a Yankee school ma'am in this county last year.
Beware lest you shear the same fate.

Regulators.

Many whites in the South objected
to the end of slavery. They were
angry to lose their cheap source of
labor and believed that white
people were truly superior. These
self-proclaimed "white supremacists"
organized hate groups, such as
the Ku Klux Klan. They used violence
to threaten and harm teachers,
freed people, and anyone who
actively set out to help black people.

Phillis Wheatley, born in Africa, was enslaved and brought to America about 1761. Her Poems on Various Subjects, Religious and Moral *was the first book written by a black woman and the second book written by an American Woman.*

THRITEENTH AMENDMENT (1865)

Section 1. Neither slavery nor involuntary servitude, except as a punishment for crime whereof the party shall have been duly convicted, shall exist within the United States, or any place subject to their jurisdiction.

FOURTEENTH AMENDMENT (1868)

Section 1. All persons born or naturalized in the United States, and subject to the jurisdiction thereof, are citizens of the United States and of the state wherein they reside. No state shall make or enforce any law which shall abridge the privileges or immunities of citizens of the United States; nor shall any state deprive any person of life, liberty, or property, without due process of law; nor deny to any person within its jurisdiction the equal protection of the laws.

FIFTEENTH AMENDMENT (1870)

Section 1. The right of citizens of the United States to vote shall not be denied or abridged by the United States or by any state on account of race, color, or previous condition of servitude.

These three amendments represented a major and radical shift in America's legal position. Although daily life remained much the same for most people, these statements influenced American policies for years to come, especially during the Civil Rights Movement in the 1960s.

The men pictured here were the first blacks to be voted into government positions. They served in the U.S. Congress.

Seated from left to right, they are:

> *Senator Hiram R. Revels of Mississippi*
> *Representative Benjamin S. Turner of Alabama*
> *Josiah T. Walls of Florida*
> *Joseph H. Rainey of South Carolina*
> *Robert Brown Elliott of South Carolina*

Standing from left to right:

> *Representative Robert C. De Large of South Carolina*
> *Representative Jefferson F. Long of Georgia*

FREE AT LAST

Jubilantly ♩ = 108

Chorus

Free at last, free at last, I thank God I'm free at last; Free at last, free at last, I thank God I'm free at last. Oh free at last.

(Solo) Way down yon-der in the grave-yard walk,

Chorus I thank God I'm free at last,

(Solo) Me and my Je-sus gon-na meet and talk, —

Chorus I thank God I'm free at last. Oh

D.C. al Fine

FREE AT LAST
(continued)

2. On my knees when the light passed by,
   I thank God I'm free at last,
   Thought my soul would rise and fly,
   I thank God I'm free at last.
   (Chorus)

3. Some of these mornings, bright and fair,
   I thank God I'm free at last,
   Gonna meet my Jesus in the middle of the air,
   I thank God I'm free at last.
   (Chorus)

Because slaves had been punished for speaking out, it became common for the words of songs to have dual meanings—one that was acceptable—and a second, hidden significance. An example is this traditional spiritual, which was jubilantly sung in black churches before and after the Emancipation Proclamation. The lyrics describe the religious act of going to heaven and celebrate freedom from the bonds of slavery.

Hard Gingerbread

Rub half a pound of butter into a pound of flour; then rub in half a pound of sugar, two table-spoons of ginger, and a spoonful of rose water; work it well; roll out, and bake in flat pans in a moderate oven. It will take about half an hour to bake. This gingerbread will keep good some time.

This recipe comes from Early American Cookery: "The Good Housekeeper," *by Sarah Josepha Hale.*

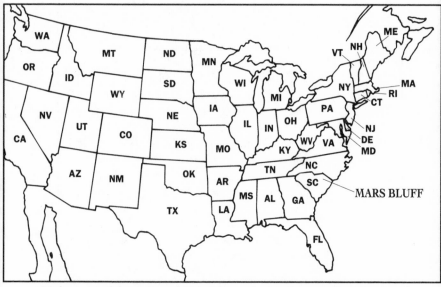

Modern map of the continental United States, showing the approximate location of Davis Hall Plantation in Mars Bluff, South Carolina, about one hundred miles north of Charleston.

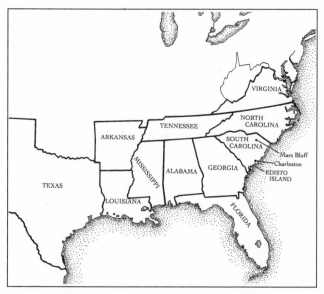

This detail shows which states permitted slavery before the end of the Civil War.

About the Author

JOYCE HANSEN is the distinguished author of two Coretta Scott King Honor books, *Which Way Freedom?* and *The Captive*, which was published by Scholastic Press. She has done extensive research and writing, both fiction and nonfiction, on the Civil War and the Reconstruction Era, and has won a Children's Book Award from the African Studies Association, as well as an Edgar Allan Poe Award.

Writing *I Thought My Soul Would Rise and Fly* evolved from a serendipitous research experience.

"A few years ago when I was writing a nonfiction book on Reconstruction, I read the diary of a woman, Emma Holmes, who had lived in Charleston, South Carolina, during and after the Civil War. In a May 1865 entry, she described a servant girl, a former slave, named Ann. She wrote that Ann was 'lame, solitary, very dull, slow, timid, and friendless.'

"The description resonated for me. I'd found one

of those little gems that I sometimes discover when doing historical research. I was fascinated by this 'timid, friendless' girl. Was she really timid and dull? Why was she friendless? What had happened to her mother and father? Had she always lived with Emma Holmes? Suppose she wasn't as mentally slow and dull as Holmes thought? What if she were actually quite bright?

"These questions couldn't be answered, for Holmes never again mentioned Ann in her diary. But I tucked Ann away in a corner of my mind and thought that maybe someday I'd create a character based on her. Three years later, I found the chance to bring her to life in this story of Patsy, a freed girl. Of course, as the diary progressed, Patsy took on a life of her own and answered all of those questions I'd once had about Ann.

"Although *I Thought My Soul Would Rise and Fly* is fictional, the details are based on the diaries, journals, oral histories, and narratives of people who lived through those tumultuous times. The catechsim that Patsy hated was an actual 'slave catechism.' But it was the description of the lame, timid, friendless girl that truly fired my imagination."

Ms. Hansen has been writing for young people for the past seventeen years. Until recently, she lived and worked in New York City, where she was born. A public school teacher of English and creative writing for twenty-two years, she now writes full time in South Carolina, where she lives with her husband. And even though she has retired from teaching, she says, "I still feel like a teacher, and when I write, I hear my students' voices, warning me not to be boring."

Acknowledgments

Grateful acknowledgment is made for permission to reprint the following:

Cover portrait: *La Negresse* by May Alcott Nieriker, sister of Louisa May Alcott, author of *Little Women*. Private collection of Tanja Ammer-Bauer, Traife, Germany.

Cover Background: *Plantation Burial* by John Antrobus, Historic New Orleans Collection, New Orleans, Louisiana.

Page 183: Children at rural cabin, Library of Congress
Page 184: Laundresses, Onondaga Historical Society, Onondaga Historical Association, Syracuse, New York.
Page 185: Cotton pickers working as "sharecroppers," New-York Historical Society, New York, New York
Page 186 (top): Oxcart with freed people, Library of Congress
Page 186 (bottom): Public wedding of freed people, Library of Congress
Page 187 (top): Meeting of Freedmen's Bureau, ibid.
Page 187 (bottom): Classroom of school for freed people, ibid.
Page 188 (top): Title page of *The History of Little Goody Two-*

Shoes, Rare Book and Manuscript Library, Columbia University, New York, New York

Page 188 (bottom): Ku Klux Klan letter, Library of Congress

Page 189: Portrait of Phillis Wheatley, ibid.

Page 191: First black United States Congressmen, Library of Congress

Page 192: "Free At Last," from *Songs of the Civil War,* compiled and edited by Irwin Silber, Dover Publications, Inc., New York, New York

Page 193 (top): Lyrics from "Free At Last," ibid.

Page 193 (bottom): Recipe for hard gingerbread, from *Early American Cookery: "The Good Housekeeper,"* by Sarah Josepha Hale, Dover Publications, Inc., New York, New York

Page 194: Maps by Heather Saunders

Other books in the *Dear America* series

A Journey to the New World
The Diary of Remember Patience Whipple
by Kathryn Lasky

The Winter of Red Snow
The Revolutionary War Diary of Abigail Jane Stewart
by Kristiana Gregory

When Will This Cruel War Be Over?
The Civil War Diary of Emma Simpson
by Barry Denenberg

A Picture of Freedom
The Diary of Clotee, a Slave Girl
by Patricia C. McKissack

Across the Wide and Lonesome Prairie
The Oregon Trail Diary of Hattie Campbell
by Kristiana Gregory

So Far from Home
The Diary of Mary Driscoll, an Irish Mill Girl
by Barry Denenberg

Copyright © 1997 by Joyce Hansen.

All rights reserved. Published by Scholastic Inc.
DEAR AMERICA®, SCHOLASTIC, and associated logos are trademarks of Scholastic Inc.

Library of Congress Cataloging-in-Publication Data
Hansen, Joyce.
I thought my soul would rise and fly: the diary of Patsy, a freed girl
Mars Bluff, South Carolina, 1865
by Joyce Hansen.
p. cm. — (Dear America; 6)
Summary: Twelve-year-old Patsy keeps a diary of the ripe but confusing time following the end of the Civil War and the granting of freedom to former slaves.
ISBN 0-590-84913-1 (alk. paper)
1. Afro-Americans — History — 1863–1877 — Juvenile fiction.
2. Reconstruction — Juvenile fiction. 3. United States-History — 1865–1898 — Juvenile fiction.
[1. Afro-Americans — History — 1863–1877 — Fiction.
2. Reconstruction — Fiction. 3. United States-History — 1865–1898 — Fiction. 4. Diaries — Fiction.]
I. Title. II Series
PZ7.H1933Iaj 1997
[Fic] — dc21   LC#: 97-2170
CIP   AC

10 9 8 7 6 5 4 3 2 1   03 04 05 06 07

The display type was set in Nicholas Cochin.
The text type was set in Cochin and Garamond Italic.
Book design by Elizabeth B. Parisi

Printed in the U.S.A. 23
First printing, October 1997

Reinforced Library Edition
ISBN 0-439-55505-1
November 2003